A]

MW01038773

Liora Barash Morgenstern

A Dog's Luck

Liora Barash Morgenstern

Translated from Hebrew by Daniella Zmir

First printed in Hebrew on September 2014 as
"Mazal Shel Kelev"

Contact: real2000@zahav.net.il

ISBN-13: 978-1539112518
ISBN-10: 1539112519

With love and longing
To my sister, Miki
Of blessed memory

"The episode…

What happened, happened…

The episode…

What happened, happened…"

Echoes within me time after time.

The echoes replay.

And become louder.

Blending together.

Doing with me as they wish.

And the silence is burdensome.

They will not let go.

Condensing.

Collapsing.

Refracting into endless traces.

Voices and silences hang their gaze upon me.

Pleading for expression.

The dust of past generations ascends.

Billowing.

Blinding.

The knot in the stomach tightens.

And the passion, too, grows.

It is now clear to me: every performance is intrinsically singular, true to insight, state of mind and temperament—of the listener as well—at a particular point in time.

I turn my back to the keyboard, the keys I frequently play.

In my mind's eye I stand on a podium.

At the front of the stage.

The spotlight is on me.

In my right hand: the pen, my conductor's baton, designed for final flourishes, to maintain continuity, rhythm and precision of expression.

With my left—the hand of emotion—I start turning the pages of my life.

The rustle is familiar.

Perhaps bestowing confidence, perhaps unsettling.

Like performers, who, as if knowing from the very beginning where they are headed, I also want to create a field of inspiration that arouses attention: to weave warps of voices into the wefts of silences in accordance to the length of their breaths. To instill content in the tempo, inner logic in emotion, or the other way around. To separate the primary theme from the secondary, and from one intermezzo or another. To follow the development of every elusive and subtle melody. To trace the interplay between figure and background—where either one is brought out by the other, or is suppressed by it. To allude to motifs before they appear and develop them from themes that will fade, only to reemerge with greater force. Wishing for music that will play by itself. For that one time when not even the trace of a foreign cell remains in the texture. And when the last chord dies out, somehow the echoes, too, will be void of existence…

I straighten my shoulders.

And drop them.

Sway my head from side to side.

Loosen my arms.

Look deeply.

Far.

And slowly slowly I begin to attune.

Hesitating how I will open:

Tempo.

Dynamics.

Scale.

Attentiveness emanates from every corner.

This is it:

This is the moment to raise the baton.

I purse my lips.

Lift my hands.

Slightly bend my elbows to refine the gestures.

Breathe in deeply.

Slowly breathe out.

Move forwards and backwards through space and time.

Hear the tone.

Give the signal.

And…

The still voice of silence.

The intensity of the attentiveness carries me back to Grandpa Danny, Mom's father, who died shortly before I turned nine. As long as he was in good health, the radio on his nightstand clattered non-stop:

"Between you and me… this is the most loyal of my acquaintances."

Once, after I nagged him to turn it off, or at least to change stations, he adjusted his heavy-framed glasses. Directed an earnest gaze.

Cleared his throat.

Cleared his throat again.

And only when I promised to keep his words to myself, he lowered his voice, even though there was no one but us in the house:

"Before bed he **bids me**… 'Good night.'

When I open my eyes he **greets me**… 'Good morning.'

With him…—**loneliness** is kept at arm's length…"

The distance of place and time emphasizes intonations that weren't there when he went out of his way to endear me to classical music, which did not speak to me at the time.

Today, when I recognize a few measures of the music Grandpa loved—Verdi's Requiem, Mahler's Third Symphony, and especially Chopin's nocturnes, "which allow us to get to know him with much greater intimacy," he would accentuate softly—I listen with one ear for Grandpa.

Sue, my most cherished dog, shuffles in with her head hanging low and her tail folded. The straw mat crackles as she slouches at the foot of the bed. Even in her old age—she knows when to keep clear.

She looks at me.

Rolls her eyes.

And closes them.

I stare out the window overlooking the lawn in the backyard and the orchard on the left, which begins next to the kitchen and stretches out to the end of the grounds.

The screensaver reflects in the glass panel.

Flickers.

Winks.

The static hum of the computer seduces and intimidates.

I want to drop the pen.

To shift the spotlight.

To step off the podium.

And the desire.

The passion.

Or God-knows-what—

Will not let go.

1

My mind wanders to Grandpa's apartment, which for years has been rented out, "Until maybe one day you'd like to live there," as Mom suggested years ago. And here I am, in my childhood home, in a village in the Sharon, Israel's northern part of the coastal plain, with a knot in my stomach, passion and echoing fragments of voices and silences that won't let go.

I rise from my executive chair, Mom's gift for the PhD I'm writing, to her pride and to the dismay of my father, who burrows through the newspapers and "Can't find any classified ads for philosophers… not to mention an expert on the metaphor…"

I walk over to the French window.

Throw it open.

Twilight intrudes.

The early fall breeze is refreshing.

Josh is barking in the yard, the youngest pup of Sue and Champion, my eldest dog who passed away at a ripe old age.

For him—I don't go out. Even in his later years—toward him I feel differently than toward his parents—all three, Groenendael Belgian Shepherds: average height, with long, smooth black fur, brown at the tips in Sue and Josh, and without that pure white furry medallion at the center of his chest, which granted his father a unique elegance. A rather pointed face. Intelligent almond eyes, brownish-black. Perked triangular ears. And my heart goes out to his father, Ron Yovel, as his name appears on the registry, and whom I called On as a toddler. And ever since, the name Ron-On has stuck.

Ron, whose achievements eventually earned him the nickname Champion, was about a year old when I was born. From the very first day, as Mom and Dad have often told me, he took me under his protection: when I cried he wouldn't let go of the hems of my parents' clothes until they came to me. When I was sick he never left my side. Only when he resumed his daily routine did my parents know I had regained my strength.

He was mischievous. Loyal. Devoted. And yet, jealous. Inconsiderate. Aggressive. Domineering. Even as an epileptic old-timer, hard of seeing and hearing, who bumped into the walls he knew so well, who wasn't always in control of his bowels and who emanated unpleasant smells, he excelled in exploiting every scrap of weakness to preserve his status. Thus, until his last day he remained an omnipotent and incontestable ruler.

What is that silence?

Josh has stopped barking.

The rustle of fall leaves crunching underneath his paws evokes the memory of the clucking of Levana the chicken and her flock. Robert the rooster, who was my childhood alarm clock. The snoring of Champion, who, at Robert's call, even in the winter, would stick his cold, moist nose under the blanket. Lick my feet and my face, and with scratching nails, race to the gate to fetch the newspaper. Place it on my father's chair and rush to squeeze himself under the table, eagerly awaiting my treats.

Once the meal was over, Champion would also embark on his daily toil: guarding me. When we tried to stop him, he would dig, crawl under the hedge, and more than once, report to his watch covered with blood.

As long as I was little, I did not mind him accompanying me almost everywhere. On the contrary.

Over time, what had once filled me with a sense of security became a nuisance.

An invasion of privacy.

Dominance.

Tyranny.

I became truly haunted only when I realized that except for Adi, my best friend from childhood (who's as crazy about dogs as I am), I was facing a problem: he was happy to see my friends as though they had come to play with him, and he would jump on them the way he leaped at us.

Tears—made no impression on him.

And even less—what I wanted.

Only one thing mattered to him:

What he wanted.

Or else, he would take revenge.

To the prickly pear bush that grew wild to the left of the gate, yielding its purple, sweet and succulent fruit every summer—he was unable to cause any damage. Nor to the bird of paradise with its sharp beak, which still blazes in front of the house. Nor to the olive and pomegranate groves, with the gray-trunked fig at the front, a thick shade tree whose notched leaves are turning white, and of which Grandpa Danny used to recite:

"About such groves it is said: 'every tree in it is pleasing to the eye and to the stomach.'"

Champion bullied the bushes: injuring the roots of the pale jasmine, the yellow white broom, the Chinese honeysuckle turning its petals from white to flushing pink and the Spanish flag, entwining in the hedge-row. Uprooted seasonal flowers. Vandalized the vegetable patch. And especially the herb garden, the apple of Mom's eye, which to this day she tends with her green thumb.

I was about seven at the time. Night after night I racked my brain over how to break free of my shadow without him taking revenge on the garden.

"…Two of each living creature entered the ark with Noah." The verse Grandpa often uttered flickered in my mind one night: that Ron-On would have a friend, and not be dependent on my favors or on those of my friends.

Once it flickered, it wouldn't let go.

And each time it made more sense to me.

Eventually I raised the suggestion at the dinner table, around which our conversations were always held.

Dad listened with a blank expression.

"Another dog is another child, not to mention the damage to the garden," he ruled.

"That's on the one hand… On the other hand, perhaps the two would keep each other company and let the garden be," Mom said and winked at me, and her face twisted in a funny way, as it always happens when she winks.

The first round of conversations was thus concluded by Mom and Dad's assurance that they would discuss the issue and get back to me.

Much more—I could not have expected.

The next rounds were virtual.

Weeks passed until that Saturday morning, when Mom announced they had decided to consult an expert:

"Yael from Safed."

"**Head** of the Belgian Sheepdog Breeders Association of Israel," Dad emphasized with an air of importance. With a floating smile she told me they had spoken to her on the phone.

And were favorably impressed.

And she was expecting us.

We embarked on our journey with Ron-On sitting tall and proud next to me in the back seat, looking out the half-open window. When I asked how she could be of help, Mom mentioned that after Ron-On's being raised as an "only child," what his reaction might be to sharing the attention, or, for instance, what would be more advisable choosing male or fe…

"Haste makes waste," Dad interrupted her. "For now we're only at the stage of gathering data, which is intended to minimize the damage of rash decisions."

After treating us to mints, which she keeps in her purse at all times, Mom wiped the beads of sweat above her upper lip. "If that were the case," she said and laughed, "we could have spared ourselves the dubious pleasure of rambling along the roads in a heat wave." My mood soared and slumped according to the level of hope, corresponding to what was directly stated and what I read between the lines.

The way to the Sea of Galilee was longer than ever: we passed by beaches that even back then had begun to expand, "Because of the drought and the subsequent drop in the water level," Dad explained. We arrived in Rosh Pina, one of the first Jewish settlements in the Upper Galilee, as Mom told me. We climbed the slope of Mt. Canaan to the outskirts of the ancient town of Safed, which greeted us kindly with its chill. When we curved along the alleyways, even Ron-On's breaths were less flat and frequent.

Suddenly he burst into barks.

Thrashed against the window.

Scratched.

Tried to leap.

Even Dad struggled to restrain him.

At the edge of one of the diverging alleys, four Ron-On lookalikes paced the fence.

He barked.

And the quartet replied in chorus.

"Quiet!" An authoritative tone, which hushed him as well, was accompanied by measured thuds of clogs growing louder and louder on the cement path.

"Yael," the pleasant-mannered woman introduced herself with an energetic voice, as the iron gate screeched against its rusting hinge.

"You're Ellie," she determined.

"And you're Ron-On," she said and patted his head through the half-open window.

The minute she opened the door,

He immediately leaped out.

Covered her with licks.

And broke into a run toward the fence.

"Stay!" she commanded him.

He stopped in his tracks.

Shook himself.

As if beside himself.

"Come!" she instructed him.

His head hanging low, he retraced his steps.

"Sit!" she ordered him.

Growling in protest, he obeyed.

"You can leave the collar in the car." Without taking her eyes off him, she half-instructed Mom, who was lingering in the car, half-reprimanded her.

Mussing his shiny fur, she admired:

"Aren't you a beauty!"

"Stand!" she commanded.

Reached out.

Groped his private parts.

"No undescended testicles," she muttered to herself.

Parted his lips. Examined his gums.

"One hundred percent purebred," she determined. "So how come you aren't members of the association?"

"Nice to meet you, Mrs. Yovel," she said and shook Mom's hand with a small smile.

"My name is Tali," Mom set the tone, and thanked Yael for making herself available to meet us on such short notice.

"Ido, nice to meet you too," Dad said and extended his hand.

"The dogs are trained. Right, Yael?"

"Me, they obey," she challenged me.

"Heel!"

Ron-On stuck to my left side.

And the four aligned to his left.

"Ellie, what can I say, you're a real Shepherds' shepherd," Yael complimented me.

Hidden at the end of the path was a small house built of black basalt, ivy intertwining along its walls. Ancient olive and walnut trees shaded the yard. And tall boughs of cypress whispered murmurs.

Mom's gaze wandered:

"Groomed dogs, sturdy trees, persistent climber plants. And what about a vegetable patch…?" she asked while wiping the soles of her shoes against the iron lattice doormat.

"With your permission, Tali, we can discuss that later. First—water for Ron. He must be dehydrated from the journey. And what about you?" she asked somewhat perfunctorily.

The visit went smoothly, mostly thanks to the hosting dogs, who were accustomed to eating and drinking in company.

Yael, who had taken notice of Ron's desire to lead, spoke at length about the females, who are usually more good-natured. And about males, who are usually more handsome ("not inevitably, in order to find favor with the females"). And especially about Belgian Shepherds, "Purebreds…"

I, who always took pride in him, never thought about how the compliments were shared between him and his breed.

At the same time I also learned that "purebred dogs" are more susceptible to illnesses that "crossbreds" suffer from immeasurably less.

And that stressed me out…

Ron-On had already suffered one epileptic seizure.

Blurriness.

Sudden stiffness.

Loss of consciousness.

Convulsions.

Spasms.

Foaming at the mouth.

Passing out for seconds, which for me were an eternity.

Even when "the episode"—as Mom referred to it, and we followed suit—was over, he was confused and his legs trembled:

When he tried to stand up, he collapsed.

When he tried to walk, he faltered.

It took him hours to recover.

Fortunately, it happened only once. And when it did happen that one time, it was after I had been playing with him outside in the heavy heat for too long. A year had since passed, and "the episode" did not recur.

It didn't bother me that Yael was left with the impression that I was wandering off because the conversation had started to bore me. The important thing was that she equipped me with a tennis ball.

When he saw how they caught it with their teeth and returned it for me to throw again, he tried to seize it: Ran around.

Tailed.

Barked.

Eventually he caught the ball.

Hid it.

And with that he brought the game to an end.

"There is no doubt the situation will improve," Yael ruled when I returned: "Ron is quite the rooster."

"Our rooster is called Robert," I joined in the conversation and triggered an outburst of laughter that embarrassed me.

Yael insisted that with a male companion, there is usually more competition. However, with a female:

"You might even get puppies…

And that's an extraordinary experience…"

Even in my doggiest dreams, I had never reached such splendors.

When she accompanied us to our car she told us that she had made some inquires, no strings attached, of course, among members of the association. And she had also phoned a colleague, a dog breeder from Belgium, who just had a litter of seven. "Madam Lauren still hasn't found a good home for one of the puppies."

She gave Mom a note with the phone number, for us to contact her if we wished.

"And don't forget to register with the association!" she yelled after us. "Especially if you decide to give him a helpmate. Not to mention if there is a whelping!"

Like us, others also turn to her, trying every which way to find "purebred puppies, with certificates."

His energy spent, Ron-On slept the entire way.

I lay beside him and tried to sort out in my mind whether pedigree was important to me.

And if so, why.

To this day I cannot settle the contradiction between "racial purity" and my dog. And yet, if I ever left home… I would obviously raise a Belgian Shepherd like him.

* * *

I dedicated the end of summer break to training:

With perfect timing he would leap and catch the ball like a juggler.

To return it—he refused.

Treats were futile.

I consulted my good girl friend Adi and we developed a method:

Tossing softly.

From up close.

Aiming for the head, so it would bounce back.

Instantly he took to the new game.

Encouraged, I imposed a training regimen:

Early in the morning, before the heavy heat.

And shortly before sunset, after it broke.

Twenty minutes, tops.

Watching his performances, Dad smiled with pleasure:

"Ron-On the champion."

And the nickname stuck to him until his last day.

The intensity of the training also made it easier for me to endure the wait, as there was no further mention of a puppy.

A short time after the school year started, Mom informed me that the puppy in Belgium had already been weaned. And that we may soon start preparing for her arrival.

In front of my parents I continued to show restraint. But when I was with Adi (who back then was still raising Tush-Tush the First, a large poodle who was run over the following year, after which she took comfort in Tush-Tush the Third, because "There could be no second to the first…") I talked her head off. To be precise: I could not talk to her about anything else.

Together we flipped through dog albums.

We dreamed.

Planned.

Fantasized.

Together we counted the days.

The hours.

And… not a single word.

One evening, when my parents brought me back from Adi's, they mentioned a surprise waiting for me at home:

"Nothing too exciting…"

My breath caught in my chest.

At home Mom went outside to pick vegetables.

Diced them finely.

And we waited.

Again she went out, returning with fistfuls oregano and basil.

And we waited.

Dad cooked my favorite pasta sauce.

And we waited.

I set the table.

And we waited.

They ate.

And we waited.

I dried the dishes he washed.

And we waited.

Mom put everything back in place.

And we waited.

We waited and waited.

God knows for what.

My heart leaped at the sound of the doorbell.

On his return, Dad was accompanied by Shlomo Zehavi, his best friend from the army:

"We served together in the paratroopers' brigade. We were in the same tent. Adjacent beds." To this day he does not miss a single opportunity to remind me.

Unlike her usual reaction, Mom's face lit up when he entered.

Mine fell.

As part of his work (which was never discussed, even in private) Shlomo frequently traveled abroad. On his way home, he often stopped by our house and showered me with gifts.

"Because for Shlomo, who never married, you're like a daughter," Dad would recite.

Apart from his small suitcase, he carried something pink and rectangular; I couldn't tell whether it was a basket or a bag. I did not like it one bit.

My parents exchanged glances.

Mom's eyes wandered back to Shlomo.

"Young Miss Yovel," he said, looking at me and addressing Mom: "It is my honor and privilege to bestow a royal gift upon you," he related with pathos as he handed me the basket-bag.

I turned pale.

My knees shook.

My mouth went dry.

And the words escaped me.

"What, aren't you curious?" he urged me.

The handles of the carrier vibrated.

The bag almost dropped when Mom stopped me to spread a newspaper on the table. When I set it down I noticed round air-holes.

Nothing was inside, apart from a black ball of wool in the corner.

"This is Suzan. As befitting a princess, she flew with style."

With restrained enthusiasm he told us that he had held her on his lap for the entire flight. And not only the passengers, but even the pilot came to look at her:

"She's one curious pup, your Suzan…"

With Mom's encouragement, I opened the basket-bag.

A stench pricked my nostrils.

"That's from the red carpet the Madam spread out for her, to absorb the pee and poop, and also to keep her warm in the car and on the air-conditioned plane," Shlomo said and laughed.

Everything was surreal.

Hallucinatory.

Bizarre.

Especially when Dad picked up the shriveled ball and placed it in my arms.

The touch was caressing.

Softer than silk.

Than angora.

Softer than soft.

And the scent—nothing was fresher.

Slowly slowly the tiny ball began to swell.

At that same moment Champion burst into sharp barks.

The barks grew stronger.

Increased in frequency.

Turned fierce.

And the ball shivered.

Flattened.

Shrank.

Dad gripped my shoulder and led the way.

Champion's fur bristled.

He barked.

And Suzan quivered.

He shook.

As if about to attack, he recoiled.

He bumped into the armchair near the television nook in the kitchen.

He squeezed under it.

And did not stop barking:

Feared and barked.

Raged and barked.

Protested and barked.

Barked and barked.

At Suzan.

At me.

At the basket-bag.

At everything and everyone.

The essential became trivial.

And the trivial—essential.

And the essential—infinitely trivial.

I lost my senses.

I was lost.

I felt sorry for him.

For her.

I felt regret.

I was overwhelmed with guilt.

He wouldn't stop.

And Suzan made not a single sound.

At her request, I handed Suzan to Mom. But even when Shlomo laughed at the spreading yellow stain, instead of changing my clothes, I approached him.

I kneeled.

Her scent preceded me.

And Champion entrenched himself deeper.

I tried talking to him.

He continued to recoil.

Gradually the barks faded.

Their frequency diminished.

And slowly the barks were replaced by grumbles, whether disapproving or complacent I couldn't tell.

"That's one hell of a guy!" admired Dad, whose style of speech and diction change to this day when Shlomo is around.

"This is his house.

And he's guarding it."

Shlomo lowered his gaze.

"That's how dogs react when **they** are threatened… strictly between ourselves," Mom mumbled, "**we**'re the same… but **they**… are lucky: **dogs** keep nothing to themselves."

From a distance of time and place I notice emphases that had eluded me when she laughed and said that if Champion hadn't reacted that way, we would really have something to worry about.

Shifting her gaze from me to Dad, she was adamant that with all the support, love and warmth we would shower them with, they would gain confidence in no time.

"What is he saying, after all?! That he's blessed with healthy instincts." As she asked, she replied: "And that he's afraid that Suzan will take his place. What could be more natural than that? More human than that?"

All at once everything came out:

"Bec…ause…of… meee…

The…y… sepa…rated…

Herrr….

Fff…rom… her… mo…ther

And fff…rom… eve…ry…thing

A…nd… fff…or

Wh…at…?!"

Dad asked that I get into my head "real good":

"There's no authority without responsibility."

Seeing that the authority to take in Sue is his and Mom's **exclusively**, he stressed, they bear the responsibility as well.

The crying increased.

Mom handed Sue to Shlomo.

Approached me.

Hugged me.

And let me cry on her shoulder.

Slowly slowly the crying turned into sobs.

The weeping gradually abated.

When they tears dried on their own, once again she implored me to go change my clothes.

When I returned I was greeted by an almost routine-like atmosphere.

Even Champion seemed less threatened.

Dad brought in his old camera and a modern video camera (among the first that came out for home use; had Mom not given it to him as a gift, I doubt he would have treated himself to one), and started memorializing.

"What do you want to do with the carrier?" she wished to know. "The pleasure is all yours." With her manicured nails she held her nose and handed me my gift.

Something shook from side to side.

I stuck my hands in:

I took out a wrapped box.

And a rubber teddy bear—pink as well.

I casually squeezed it. Her puppish ears, which were still dropped, trembled at the squealing sound.

Shlomo placed Suzan on the newspaper sheets with which Mom had padded the oilcloth she spread out on the table.

And I—the teddy bear.

Suzan stood up to her full tiny height.

And then she was revealed in all her splendor:

A delightful tiny teddy bear.

In the presence of the toy again, it was as if the cry of infancy had brought her closer to a faraway home.

And when it escaped her, she chased it from one end of the table to the other.

Champion did not take his eyes off her.

And did not miss a gesture—hers or ours.

Mom brought out new bowls.

And offered Suzan a bit of water.

"Suzan…" I hesitated.

"That name… isn't it a size too big on her?

She's more of a Sue, don't you think…?"

"After Sue drinks," Mom went along with the new name, "we'll wait. If she doesn't throw up, we'll offer her something to eat. She must be starving."

"How did you know?!" Shlomo was astonished. And said that the Madam had cautioned him not to feed her a single crumb, so she wouldn't vomit. "And with all the groupies gathered around her with all kinds of goodies—it was one hell of a challenge."

Sue licked gently.

Took a break.

And resumed her licking.

When she went back to playing with the teddy bear, Mom asked my permission, just to be on the safe side, to let them separate the dogs for the first few nights:

Sue would sleep with her and Dad.

And Champion—as always, with me.

In the meantime I tore the wrapper off a box of dog food.

I handed Dad the pink envelope that was inside.

Shlomo, who is fluent in French, translated a letter from September 30, 1987, the eve of Sue's arrival, addressed to all of us, and especially to me:

Madam Lauren introduced herself as a well-experienced breeder, and Suzan—who, together with her six siblings, came into the world on July 22, 1987—hailing from a grand lineage: she inherited her Parisian coquettishness from her mother, who was a French champion. And she directed our attention to notarized copies confirming her French descent, copies of the championships her father won, of her lineage, and of a document stating that there is no blood relations between her parents.

Her name starts with the letter S, she explained, because in Belgium once a year the first letter of the names of Belgian Shepherd newborns is announced, in alphabetical order. Coincidentally, it was the nineteenth whelping in her breeding kennel, corresponding to the letter S in the Latin alphabet.

And she gave us her word that she had not addressed her by any name until she was given permission by my parents. And she had since allowed herself to call her by the pet name Sue.

She described Sue as good-natured. Kind. Friendly. And she did not hide how difficult the separation was for her.

She detailed what she ate, how much and when. And added that in order to ease her acclimation, she was also sending along her favorite toy, saturated with the taste of home, and a box of the dry food she had accustomed her to eat prior to the departure. She instructed us to give her a bit of water. And if she didn't throw up, to offer her a little food as well. And to take her out to the yard immediately because she still had the occasional indoor accident.

She pleaded with us not to expect Ron to rejoice in her arrival. And she guaranteed that if we let him adjust, within a short period he would start enjoying his helpmate. After all, there is no greater gift!

Ending her letter, she wrote that she had pups around the world, from the Ivory Coast to Japan. And she would be grateful if from time to time we would update her on her development. And if possible, preferably on video.

Even the beating of a mosquito's wings could have been heard when he folded the letter.

Mom was moved by Madam Lauren's love for Sue and how well she understood her…

And as if to herself, she mumbled that we all would have been spared quite a bit of grief had we found the letter first. Dad did not stop admiring how well she had coped with the separation… And Shlomo was excited by the Madam, who had driven herself all the way to Orly Airport and back. And he told us that because of how she had "kept her cool…" he too saved face.

Before he left, he remembered a gift she had sent for Champion.

He sniffed the beef-flavored shoe with suspicion.

And did not touch.

The moment we looked away, he charged at it.

Sank his teeth into it.

And shook it playfully.

* * *

The silence is broken.

Sue pushes the door open.

I didn't even notice she had left.

She stands in the doorway.

Looking hither and thither.

And slouching on the floor.

I leave the panels of the French window gaping wide.

Approach the library.

Pull out Sue's album.

Place it on the desk.

And sit back down on my executive chair.

The screen flickers.

The computer whispers.

Seduces.

I hug the album.

Stand up.

Sit on the edge of the bed.

Take off my slippers.

Stretch my legs.

Turn my back on the sorcerous computer. Rest the album in my lap.

It's a bit chilly.

Especially at my feet.

I cover them with the blanket.

And also my back.

I lean the pillow against the built-in linen chest at the head of the bed.

I burrow under the blanket.

Only the top of the nose peeks out.

As if Sue has made up her mind:

She rises with trembling feet.

And slowly staggers toward me.

Rests her head on the bed.

Absentmindedly my fingers glide across her, stroking and tapping her fur, which is to this day the silkiest.

Sue succumbs to the pleasure.

Glances at me.

And half collapses, half detaches.

I open the album and start skimming Madam Lauren's letter, then the genealogy records, the notarized copies of her father's championship certificates and the document confirming no blood relations between her parents. With my baton I point at Shlomo Zehavi, Dad's best friend from the army: "We served together in the paratroopers brigade," the tone of his voice plays within me, "we were in the same tent. Adjacent beds." I study Mom's countenance… and Dad's expression… I look at the basket-bag and find it difficult to believe that Sue was once so tiny, she disappeared inside it.

And of their own accord the photos take me back to the days in which, in order to prevent fits of jealousy, we let them stay together under Mom or Dad's watchful eye. And to the first nights during which Sue whimpered on the other side of the wall, in my parents' bedroom. And to Champion, who entered my room to sleep beside me with an eagerness that grew with every passing night, as if preserving a piece of paradise that was no longer his alone.

It was the perfect arrangement for me as well. Not only did it allow me to devote more attention to him, but it also had a more prosaic benefit: it spared me the unpleasantness of waking up to a puddle.

In my mind's eye I continue to follow Sue, who grew from one day to the next and became a spirited teddy bear, vibrant and full of joie de vivre. And from one day to the next we became acquainted with her temperament, which turned out to be wonderfully adaptive: even when her toy was snatched, she raced to retrieve it on nimble legs and with a light heart.

And subsequently, she soon realized that all he wanted was to play with her.

In fact, she found everything an amusement.

And it wasn't long before Champion, who remained terribly suspicious until his last day, also found joy in his new toy.

At first, when we let them out, she would rush behind him with tiny steps. And within a mere few days she turned into his shadow: wherever he went, she quickly followed.

When he deterred her with a sharp bark, she halted.

Looked hither and thither.

Regained her composure.

And resumed the chase.

And he realized he had someone to control.

And he liked it.

Within a short period such harmony existed between them that Mom returned to her regular work hours in the office.

He would provoke her.

And she was in constant pursuit, without standing a chance of catching up, as fast as her steps were.

When she lagged behind, he slowed down. Lurking.

And once she caught up with him, her red tongue sticking out and vibrating from shortness of breath, he would pin her down.

Toss her onto her back.

And play with her as if she were his toy.

And she cooperated: allowed him to roll her from side to side, and from stomach to back. Every now and then a sudden sob, just like a baby's, escaped her parted lips, which still hold traces of their old smile.

In fact, it was the only way he learned to gauge his strength.

To our responses—he was immune.

More than once I suspected that apart from expressing happiness from jumping on us, he enjoyed stirring up a reaction that was rarely delayed. And the facts speak for themselves: as long as he was physically up to it, he jumped on anyone on any occasion, except for two:

Sue—whom he treated with extreme caution in her puppyhood.

And Grandpa—whom he followed devotedly in his old age.

While they were still scouting their way around the first steps of sharing, when we called them in, he would immediately obey:

First he.

And she in his footsteps.

When she reached adulthood, they lingered about until they finished their business. And invariably, up until he passed away, when the duo was kind enough to finally come inside, he maintained his right of way. And if, heaven forbid, she preceded him, he would give her a good shake:

"Don't you dare forget who's in charge here."

He—who until his last day did not realize that his place was forever preserved, whose aggression was unacceptable, unnecessary and infuriating—as if clarified to her in a language that could not be defied.

In accordance with the pattern instilled in her as a puppy, when "our gallant lady," as Grandpa called her, arrived ahead of time, she would wait. And in the twilight of his life, when he was a fumbling old timer, she would lead Champion to the door and let him enter first.

The more she clung to him, the more he lost interest in the company of my friends, and the less he cooperated during our training sessions, which even Doctor Yehoram, the vet, deemed vital:

When I called him, he would turn his tail to me.

And if he complied, it was as if he was doing me a favor.

In contrast, Sue perked up at the sight of a ball.

And once I threw him the ball, she would commence chasing his tail .

Why did she do that?

God knows.

To settle a score?

Unlikely.

To gain control of the ball?

She never took interest in it on any other occasion.

To put an end to the game, as he did at the time with his lookalikes?

By her very nature, or perhaps as a result of the way she was raised, she was less competitive than he was, and far more lenient.

I tend to believe that she simply viewed this tailing as a new game. But even if she had wanted them to, her tailings never granted her the opportunity to touch it:

The ball was his.

And his alone.

And he defended his rights with uncompromising zeal.

After he passed away, the structure of their relationship had become part of her. The young pup Josh took his place and put up with her tailings, which she transferred to him as long as her body was sound and able.

And I—who am convinced that one of the most undervalued traits is attentiveness; and who so yearn for a true friend, someone who will be attentive to me in every sense, and who will stir within me the desire to be attentive to him; and who often feel lonely and detached during the process of writing my doctoral dissertation, and "without anyone that I could really talk to," like the Little Prince, who, when his plane crashed in the Sahara, was "more isolated than a ship-wrecked sailor on a raft in the middle of the ocean"— am now sensitive to every nuance of a relationship. And it is not impossible that it is my acute sensitivity that grants further prominence to other strident variations: always, and without exception, he would stick his nose in her plate, when his brimming plate was waiting just for him.

He adopted this practice upon her very first breakfast:

As a fully grown dog he ate one meal a day.

Once he saw the puppy food, he left not a single crumb.

And Sue stood.

And watched.

While she was still a puppy, he did this every day.

Three times a day:

Morning.

Noon.

And evening.

And not even once did his gluttony, provocations, or god knows what, disrupt her peace or rush the pace of her refined licks, the way she still eats to this day.

When we put him outside, he would scratch the door in a frenzy.

And the moment we let him back in, he would pummel her:

Knock her down like a sack of potatoes.

And teach her what's what.

Finally letting her rise, he would climb on top of her high-handedly. Grip her lower body with his legs. Pin her down. And half-riding-half-prostrating, as if saying:

"A bite is a bite.

But I'm the boss."

When she grew up and we switched her to two meals a day, we divided his as well.

In vain.

An entire lifetime the duo lived together:

Slept with me in my room.

Played.

In time, mated.

Bore pups.

Ate once a day.

The same food.

At the same time.

From identical plates.

He always devoured, or at least sampled, hers first.

And Sue, in her submissiveness, her survival instinct or her fear of the authority he imposed on her, acted as if it was not about her.

To this day it happens that she approaches.

Waits.

As if remembering.

And complies.

And there was another variation on the same theme, which became firmly set over time: every morning I give a grown dog a beef bone.

"It's his toothbrush," Mom taught me when I was little.

He made a fuss over this as well.

And she, as if internalizing: when I called her she would clear the path for him, since for her, in each and every matter, he was always unequivocally first.

For his part, he treated her like an available playmate, who surrenders to his whims and accepts his authority on his home court.

And although he never treated her as "bone of his bones and flesh of his flesh," when she grew up and went into heat, he demanded "to become one flesh." It was a singular episode. It had bearings on the vegetable patch, and especially on the herb garden, which, shortly before giving birth, she used to dig up, but not on their relationship, which was already established.

Since history is not a zipper that can be run back and forth, I can't hazard an educated guess as to the kind of relationship she would have instituted, if at all, had she had the opportunity to shape it to her own needs. Always, and without exception, she treated him like a privileged and omnipotent leader.

The facts speak for themselves: she never tried to run away. Was almost always happy to see him. And in his old age she guarded his privileges, large or small, and preserved his status, which he did not give up fighting for until his last day.

Another variation, and no less dissonant, was that he, for his part, never took in stride any of her achievements, and this stemmed from jealousy: from the very first moment, he reacted to any manifestation of affection toward her as if it came at his expense. And rushed to nudge her away and take her place.

This variation also took different shapes and forms, all of them sharing one theme: he couldn't bear the fact that she succeeded in doing something he was incapable of. For him it was the end of the world. And it was instantly translated into aggression.

She was exposed to the harshest manifestations of his feelings when she grew up, and had something to show off.

And it happened when the renovation was completed.

* * *

Like the rest of the houses in the village, ours was small and comprised of one floor, without a spare room for guests, who in any case almost never spent the night.

I never knew Mom's mom: "What happened, happened…" and she passed away before I was born. Apart from that Mom told me nothing about Grandma Michaela, nor did I ask.

Grandma Gertrude and Grandpa Gustav, Dad's parents, spoke only German. When Dad was in the army they sold the foreign language bookshop they owned in Tel Aviv, paid back debts and returned to Berlin. Upon visits, which became even rarer and briefer over time, only Mom and I would meet them at the hotel in the city of Netanya where they were staying, not far from our village.

When Adi slept over, we would open my bed.

On the rare occasions when Grandpa Danny was willing to forgo his own bed, in his own house, we would offer him a bed in the enclave between my parents' and my bedrooms and the bathroom.

Sue was a little over a year old when Grandpa started to drag his feet and occasionally talk nonsense, and I never knew whether to laugh or cry. Apart from Fridays, when he "spent time with the housekeeper," every day, before and after work, Mom would stop by his house. She didn't even trust Dad. On Saturdays she would leave Champion to protest alone at home, because he didn't know how to behave and she worried that, god forbid, he might jump on Grandpa or break something.

At the threshold of his apartment we were greeted by the weekend newspapers, noticeably untouched.

"I did not yet have the opportunity to dispose of them," he would make an excuse.

The radio no longer played, either.

"After all, I am no stripling," he would reply in his flowery language and a low voice, when we inquired about his well-being.

Grandpa preferred "the city a thousand times over the country," and lived in an apartment on the third floor of a building on Tel Hai Street in Tel Aviv, not far from the main square named after Zina Dizengoff.

It happened that he left.

And didn't return.

Fortunately, one of the neighbors noticed his absence.

Called Mom.

Who alerted Dad.

And the housekeeper.

Called the police.

The doctors.

Every hospital in the city.

And in all the metropolitan area.

Eventually he came back on his own, and did not understand what all the commotion was about.

But he also had no idea where he had been or what he was doing…

Since then Mom became restless.

And the constant running around exhausted her.

One evening, when she returned home as pale as can be, Dad suggested that she invite Grandpa to spend the weekend at our house.

"Out of the question," she quoted Grandpa the next day:

"He has his own home. Acquaintances with whom he dines from time to time and exchanges opinions over a cup of tea. The rural surroundings are foreign to him. Detached from the pulse of life. And the silence is deafening. And besides, he isn't comfortable at our place…"

At night I eavesdropped on the conversation on the other side of the wall, as I did every now and then. I often wonder if they ever eavesdropped on me as well. And I blush at the thought of how they would have reacted, had they known…

Mom spoke about Grandpa; no one knew better than Dad that he had been both a father and a mother to her. She spoke about the music he no longer listened to. About the phone which no longer rang. And about the feeling that kept her awake at nights, that apart from his housekeeper he did not exchange a word with a single living soul. Certainly not with the doctors… Dad shared her concern about his condition.

Even without knowing what "prognosis," "dementia" or "C.T." meant, it was clear to me: no good could come out of it.

I listened attentively, but before bedtime she preferred not to discuss it further. With a velvety voice she wondered whether Dad did not think it was time to realize their old dream and build a second floor.

More than the possibility of having a bedroom with three sided ventilation, Dad liked the idea of a walk-in closet, in which the clothes would not wrinkle, sparing him the need to press a white shirt each morning for his appearances in court. As for a study, "which would also serve as a family room," she hastened to add, he hesitated whether it would be wise to bring work home. Discussing my room, he agreed that I was already starting to outgrow it, and that if they were to renovate it, they might as well furnish it for an adolescent.

The pleasant harmony satisfied my curiosity.

I folded the pillow and plumped it as I always do.

And from one moment to the next my eyelids grew heavy.

Before sleep subdued me I still managed to hear her casually asking his opinion about designating their current bedroom for Grandpa.

His answer—I no longer heard.

"I haven't heard you say a single word about Dad!" a heated tone severed the threads of my sleep.

"I told you a thousand times! But even without my saying," he added, the impatience evident in his voice, "you know very well that your father's health worries me too."

"I learned firsthand long ago: when you talk about **my father**…—it never bodes well," she said angrily.

Thus I was exposed for the first time to the sounds that take place behind closed doors. The routine to which I woke up left no room for doubt:

It is a brief interlude melody.

An intermezzo and nothing more.

The next day I pressed my ear against the wall again: she spoke at length about Grandpa, who, in his condition, was more than anything in need of regular meals, nutritious food and sound sleep, without the soot and clamor of buses. Dad made me laugh when talking about the "castles in the sky" she was building, that would only add to her distress.

"Don't be condescending!"

The tones began to scale.

"I'm a simple man.

Tell me straightforwardly:

Where are you going with this?"

Mom couldn't understand how he had "the audacity to lecture her about straightforwardness," when he himself was "beating around the bush":

First ignoring.

Then evading.

And finally putting it all on her shoulders.

And she could not grasp how it was at all possible that he, who in his kindness, without thinking twice, would have taken in any stray dog, but when it came to her own father applied such a "double standard…"

I was not the only one.

Dad also didn't understand what this was about.

And I understood even less when he made the distinction between not turning back on the turned off switch of a respirator and pulling the plug on that same machine that "sustains the life of a dy…"

"Ido, what can I say… what can I say…?!

Deathly ill, just what I needed right now…" she sighed.

The apology was of no use.

His willingness to take back his words only fanned the flames:

"What is this?!

What's happening here?!

Words are bounced checks:

First you issue and then you cancel…?!"

From my current viewpoint, against my will I linger on the metaphor "words are bounced checks," and struggle not to wander to other realms. And go back to being attentive to the heavy silence that panted on the other side of the wall.

"You argue with one goal: to win.

And then your logic overshadows the emotion."

And with a small voice added:

"With me…" she paused, "it's actually exactly the same, but the other way around. And that's not always for the best either."

I was lost even before that.

It was more than enough for me.

I turned my back to the wall. Champion and Sue fell asleep before the argument broke out.

On one of those nights they spoke in one voice about fits of forgetfulness that could happen at any moment, day or night.

She would not hear about a nursing home.

About bringing in a stranger, as a daughter, and as an expert in human resources—there was nothing to talk about.

And Dad had no other suggestions.

"Should I understand from this that you're vetoing the suggestion?" she demanded to know.

Dad spoke about Grandpa, that his condition—which kept her awake at night—was affecting me. Him. Their relationship. "And it doesn't benefit Dad's health. Nature takes its course. And if…" they were fortunate to grow old together, they too would make every effort neither to cause grievance nor to burden me. And he wanted to hope that I would be level-headed enough to understand that's "The way of the world."

"There are all kinds of worlds…" she muttered, "and there are all kinds of sons and daughters…"

On **that subject**… even from her he would not hear a **single word!**

I was not the only one who woke up bleary-eyed. Champion, running back and forth between them, only irritated them more with "his unbearable rest-lessness."

The tension did not alleviate in the evenings either: the First Palestinian Intifada was at its peak. The confrontations with those who threw stones and Molotov cocktails spread "like wildfire," as I learned from the conversations at the dinner table, during which they always made sure to discuss only matters on which they saw eye to eye.

Time flew by, until the evening when Dad shared their decision with me:

We will build a second floor.

And every now and then offer Grandpa to stay over.

During the renovation the contractor installed a multi-level scaffold.

Champion climbed up and down it like a circus acrobat.

Once they cast the staircase and the floor was completed, we went up loaded with packages.

To Dad's whistle, Sue ran up.

Champion froze in his tracks.

I walked down with Dad.

His fur bristled like that of a petrified cat.

Sue stuck her head out.

Barked whimsically.

And he did not react.

"Something happened to him…" Mom diagnosed. "He probably slipped in our absence, got a good scare, and now he's afraid of his own shadow…"

Dad slid his arms under the Champion's stomach.

And pulled him up.

He shook.

And slumped back down.

"Let him be," she begged:

"There's no other way with anxieties…"

Sue darted downstairs.

He rose.

Pinned her underneath him.

Tossed her on her back and barked:

"In this house," as if making his point in an unequivocal language, "what I can't do, you won't do either."

Ever since, she did not climb the stairs in his presence.

At Grandpa's she continued to go up and down the stairs like an angel on Jacob's Ladder. In time, when she was in heat and we removed him to a kennel, she went back to prancing along the staircase like "a doe set free" at home as well.

2

Slowly slowly the voices begin to fuse.

The silences, too.

I wait until the last of the echoes dies out.

The room is dark.

And it suits me.

The chill, too.

Especially the stillness.

The pen, my baton, an inseparable part of me.

A natural extension, empowering and clarifying.

And I, who begin to see that which is before me, recoil.

I want to take a breath.

To pause.

And everything presses.

And everything is accelerating:

Onward!

Onward!

Sliding or perhaps tripping between scales, my mind is set on the house. From the moment it stopped being a construction site, our lives resumed their normal course: Champion stopped barking at the workers, at the cement mixer and at every passing truck. Sue recovered from the half-melancholic-half-depressive apathy she had been afflicted with throughout the entire renovation. And Champion went back to tyrannizing her as usual.

In no time, my parents forgot that their bedroom had once been downstairs. And I enjoyed my privacy in the renovated, refurnished room.

We were all in my room when Sue rose to her feet. And I noticed with panic a blood stain left behind her, which spread across the light colored carpet.

Mom, and with slightly more elaboration, Dad, let me understand that it was a sign that from now on she could have puppies. But, she was too young, and had yet to fully develop.

"And the time has not yet come…"

Champion went haywire:

As if with the touch of a magic wand his whims were forgotten.

At once the tables had turned.

And a new balance of power was created.

He became her shadow, literally:

Wherever she lay down, he sniffed.

Wherever she stood, he stooped.

Wherever she went, he climbed on top of her.

Without a shred of passion.

No sensuality. Courtship.

Kinship.

Intimacy.

It was necessity.

A force of nature.

Fatal attraction.

Sue, for her part, did not cooperate:

Did not yield to him.

And she did not yearn for him.

On the contrary, she treated him as a nuisance:

When he chased her, she would duck.

When he lay in wait, she would sit down.

And when pressed, she bore her teeth.

Only then did we learn that she knew how to stand, or rather sit, her ground.

And he, more aroused than ever, would wait for the next opportunity.

"As if possessed…

He won't let go!

He won't let her be!"

Mom was tormented.

"It's torture for him,"

Dad felt sorry for Champion.

On the eighth day, before ovulation began, we removed him to the kennel.

When he was brought back, he resumed his lordly ways.

Two or three times she went into heat. And then it was as if she was fading and losing her joy of life: fat, cumbersome and bent over, she tailed the one with the straight back, the perked tail, the one as proud as a peacock.

"She's isn't that happy here with us anymore," I shared with Mom, who wondered how I had arrived at such a far-reaching conclusion. And she went on to talk about Champion, who was lucky, because another dog would have put him in his place long ago.

"Why is Sue so down?" I asked as we sat around the table.

"Dad will let you in on a secret…" Mom said, perhaps manipulating him, perhaps giving him the go ahead.

"It's not that exactly, but rather…" she transposed the tune to him.

"…She's pregnant, and will soon whelp," Dad said, clenching his jaw and running his fingers through his hair.

"How soon is 'soon'?" I was beside myself with joy.

Pregnancy is a process that takes a little over two months, she explained. To be precise: sixty-three days. And they had wanted to shorten my wait. Now, when it was a matter of days, they had made up their mind to tell me.

I immediately phoned Adi, who was no less excited than me.

When Robert crowed the next day, I had already completed my morning chores and had one leg out the door. Adi had also arrived early to school, and said that she was given permission to come home with me so as not to miss the whelping.

At the sound of the bell we sped home.

As always, Champion jumped on us at the gate.

Licked my neck.

And did not neglect Adi.

Sue waddled heavily behind him.

The next day she also dragged her feet.

When she reached the gate, she barely offered a wag. And instead of burrowing in the herb garden, whose chill granted her shelter from the heat wave brought on by the whims of late summer verging on fall, she took refuge in the shade of the fig leaves at the entrance of the grove behind the kitchen.

Champion tasted her food.

And devoured his.

Sue—would not even touch her water.

Finally another school day ended.

Once again she shuffled to the gate. And returned to her new spot.

Ignored the water.

At the sight of her food she buried her head in the sand.

Right away I called Mom:

"Her nose is moist," I reported.

Once her mind was put at ease, she told me how she had suffered during the heat waves when she was carrying me, much earlier in her pregnancy than Sue, and without a coat of black fur.

The air was fresh and crisp after the first rain that fell during the night, but throughout the day it became extremely hot.

Mom, coming home early, parked the car on the side of the road.

When, with Adi's help, we finished clearing, cleaning and sterilizing the garage, to which there was access from the kitchen as well as from the yard, darkness had already descended.

That night we got them acquainted with the new place. Had it not been so spotless, we wouldn't have noticed the trail of mud Sue left behind. Champion's paws were spick and span.

In the morning Sue woke up full of energy, and did not even stop to sniff the slice of pastrami, her favorite food then as it is now.

Salivating, Champion lingered between my legs. Grabbed.

And devoured.

"Enough is enough," Mom ruled.

The puppies in her womb are consuming whatever is vital for their development. And if things carry on like this, she'll weaken. And so close to the whelping, this is, to say the least, undesirable.

She asked me to update her upon my return home from school. And if there was no change, "Doctor Yehoram will see her today."

Absentmindedly, she touched her nose again before leaving for work.

And went on her way.

With the sound of bell, we snatched up our backpacks.

And ran.

Champion greeted us as usual.

Sue waddled like a fattened goose.

Mom walked in shortly after us.

And Dad followed.

The vet didn't answer.

Cell phones were still rare and expensive at the time, and Dad left him a message to urgently call home or the beeper.

The beeper caught us in Netanya. We squeezed into a public telephone booth for Dad to call him back, and heard about a Golden Retriever that had been injured in a car accident:

"So there's no way you can make it before eight," Dad repeated, so we too could hear the vet's reaction.

The sun was close to setting when we opened the gate. Champion welcomed us with leaps.

"Where's Sue?!" I shouted.

"Sue! S-ue! S-u-ue!"

With his characteristic calm, especially in stressful situations, Dad asked me to maintain my composure.

"She's probably where she was in the afternoon," Adi guessed:

"There, under the fig tree."

"S-ue! S-u-u-ue!" I screamed.

Dad asked me to control myself.

"Sue always answers.

I'm telling you:

Something happened to her."

"Come on already. Move!" Adi rushed me.

My feet were rooted in place.

Refused to uproot.

Wagging his tail, Champion continued to circle us, even when I finally managed to move my feet.

Adi ran forth.

And I followed in her footsteps.

Dad bent over the pit.

Short of breath, Mom caught up with us.

"Congratulations, Sue." As if through the veil of a dream, a monotonous tone reached me: "And to you too, Champion. Sue gave birth. Sue has puppies. Don't touch Sue."

Adi ran to the garage to bring a sheet. And in the silence that prevailed, feeble bleats emanated from the pit, like kittenish yowls.

"Sue is a good dog. Sue is a great dog. Sue is a mother now. Congratulations, Sue. And to you too, Champion." Dad spread out the sheet, and continued to talk in the same rhythm, without changing his pitch or volume: "Everything is okay. Everything is okay."

The teeth she bore shone in the dim light when he laid a hand on the sheet.

Held it there.

Slowly slowly began to gently smoothen the sheet.

Slid his hand in deep.

Fondled.

Groped.

And in her weakness, she was about to bite him.

"Everything's fine. Sue is just protecting her puppies. Open your hands."

Lifted a kind of shoelace.

And placed it in my arms.

And another—in Adi's hands.

Crouched again.

And straightened up carrying Sue, the fringes of her sticky fur curdled with blood.

In her complete weariness he laid her down on the blanket Mom had spread out in the garage. And by her side, he placed what Adi and I had been holding: tadpoles with enlarged stomachs and stringy legs and the tails of field mice in a murky, unidentifiable color.

Sue stood up.

Wobbled.

Lay back down again.

And moved about restlessly.

Dad disappeared.

And rushed back with five others, slightly larger, from the same dubious family: they bore no resemblance to their mother, who had transformed from a ball of wool into a beautiful silken teddy bear. And I couldn't understand how such a captivating mother like her and such an elegant father like him could have produced such ugly puppies.

Dad took off again.

And returned equipped with the new video camera and the old still camera.

"They're completely bald.

And their tails… long as a shoelace…

Maybe you got mixed up?"

He pointed at Sue who pressed against the pups:

"I can get mixed up. She—can't."

Moist-eyed, Mom explained that in the womb the body temperature is more or less steady. And in order to ease their acclimation Sue was warming them. And she reminded me that when we had gotten Sue she was six weeks old. And she was confident that in no time I would see the tiny ones look like a real "copy of their parents."

Back and forth Champion measured the borders of the blanket, as if calling our attention to the fact that he, too, was present.

I extended my hand.

And he came running.

He did not go near the pups.

Nor did he approach Sue, who acted as if he did not exist.

"Enough!

You took photos.

You filmed.

You have enough!

I feel sorry for her…"

Mom begged for mercy on Sue.

"It's for Madam Lauren!"

He stopped clicking and settled for filming.

At eight o'clock the vet called and said that the Golden Retriever was in critical condition.

He wanted to know what was happening. And was happy that everything had gone well.

Toward the end of the conversation, Dad asked how to help her:

"If we can't just sit quietly, we can blot the blood. The most important thing is not to disturb. Sue knows exactly what to do," he repeated the vet's instructions, so we too would hear. "And since everything is going by the book, you will only arrive early in the morning."

When the house fell asleep, I tiptoed into the garage:

All night she warmed them.

Licked.

Nursed.

She did not even go out to pee.

Their feeble whimpers and her vigorous licks merged into tender sounds of initial attempts at nursing and stifled gulps.

The longer I looked, the more details I observed:

Perfect paws.

Miniature fingernails.

Even genitals.

Champion, who greeted me, would not leave my side.

Like a shadow he followed me.

When I rushed off to brush my teeth, shower and change clothes, he remained at his post.

I greeted the vet, Doctor Yehoram, at the gate.

The others waited for him in the garage.

"She tended to them all night," I filled him in, "but she hasn't eaten or drunk in two days."

"The wonders of nature," he said and laughed. "Like any healthy dog, she sensed that the whelping was near. So that she wouldn't have to leave them for the first day or two, even to move her bowels, she stopped eating and drinking. In the meantime they'll become stronger and their body temperature will stabilize."

"Young Miss Yovel," he addressed me: "when everything is in order, nature is usually smarter than all of us.

And where did she dig a hole?" he inquired.

Dad told him about the mud.

"Well, of course," the vet said and laughed. "She prepared a hole in order to give birth, and later to warm the pups."

And while speaking, he slid his fingers into a pair of gloves in order to "See what we have here."

"Three males and four females," I declared.

"We're about to see. Remember, you said four males and three females."

I realized he was pulling my leg, and yet I still left no room for error.

Before taking off his gloves, he squeezed every nipple to make sure there was milk and no blockage. And while doing so he offered Adi and me to be assistants in his clinic.

"Thank you. But no thank you.

We're busy with our own things now.

When we have time, we'll think about it," I promised.

"Strong words," Mom said, impressed.

"What does Grandpa Danny always say?

'Charity begins at home'…"

As he tossed out the gloves and was about to leave, she asked if he had any special instructions for us.

"Make sure that she takes care of herself. Although a healthy dog like her already knows that."

Once he left, Mom called her father.

The excitement swept him into the eye of our elation.

The following day she stayed home to supervise.

The moment Dad returned from work, she went to bring Grandpa over.

Even though she had always followed Grandpa adoringly, Sue growled even at him.

Despite our reprimanding him, Champion maintained a high morale.

Seized the blanket.

And went out to the yard.

Every now and then poked his nose around.

Sniffed.

Sneezed.

And disappeared as quickly as he had appeared.

"What a marvelous sight.

What a marvelous sight."

Grandpa mumbled like a worn-out soundtrack, and the longer he stood there, the more he shook like a palm frond. For a split second Sue's gaze sharpened when Dad went to get him a chair. And once again glazed over when she realized that no one was moving any closer to her pups.

"These teensy-weensies have a bigger effect on you than Ido, Ellie and me together." Glittering rays the likes of which I had never noticed before flickered in Mom's cheerful laughter.

With a frayed and stained handkerchief Grandpa wiped his forehead, and took the tease in good spirit.

He wrested himself from his chair. And slowly drew himself up to his full height, which back then had already begun to shrink.

When she started preparing dinner, Mom asked us to show Grandpa the room we had renovated for him.

Dad supported his elbow.

Grandpa gripped my hand, and as he dragged his feet we slowly advanced.

"It's beginning to look like a young lady's room…" he remarked as we passed by the entrance to my room:

"Oh well…

Once upon a time…"

His voice petered out.

"And where's Grandpa?"

Mom interrogated us upon our return.

"Until we call him to the table, he's resting in his room. And you won't believe it: he even agreed to spend the night," Dad bragged.

Her eyes narrowed into slits.

"I won't believe it…?!"

She paused.

And while casually straightening out her perfectly pressed apron, she adamantly insisted that he had agreed first and foremost to spare her the burden of driving into town again, biting off another chunk of the credit.

"And Sue and the pups also have something to do with it: they brought back memories…" she said, subtracting yet another piece.

* * *

That night Grandpa Danny broke in his new room, which, with its double bed, indirect lighting and adjacent bathroom, did not fall short of a luxurious hotel room. The breeze, free of smog and the soot of buses, without honks and screeching tires, imbued him with a sense of calm. He couldn't remember when he had last slept so peacefully, as he himself admitted wholeheartedly in the morning.

"If you weren't as stubborn as a mule, you could have already enjoyed several such nights."

Mom winked at me, and, as always, her face twitched in that same funny way.

Biting his lips he admired the wood-paneled library (whose design Mom had labored over at nights and on Saturdays). And he described how before retiring to his bed he dimmed the light of the floor lamp, which he instantly recognized as a work of Shlagman, the copper artist from Jerusalem (which had turned up at the flea market in Jaffa after a lengthy search, and hurried to match to it a lampshade from fine parchment). The shutters obeyed him, and rose with the touch of the switch. And he sat down to read in the rocking chair. Every so often looked up at the sky, and it seemed to him as if "all the stars were laughing."

Upon returning from school I found him hunched in the chair in the garage, far enough from the blanket. His chin rested on his thumb, clasped in his index finger.

When he noticed me he rubbed his eyes, jiggled his heavy-framed glasses and found it hard to believe that "before it even began, the school day had already ended."

"I cannot take my eyes off of Sue, who has not yet eaten even a crumb," his tone carried compassion and concern, "off her and her magnificent seven."

And he went on praising Sue, who had transformed overnight from "being as free as a bird" to a mother "in every fiber of her body and soul." And he dedicated words for Champion as well, who "from time to time calls upon them. As if making sure that everything is in order. And disappears as quickly as he appears."

Pushing his glasses up the bridge of his nose, he drew my attention to the fact that some of the teensy-weensies were bigger than others. Probably they had been the first to emerge. But he was keeping an eye especially "on the tiny lad…"

"Lady,"

I corrected him:

"She was probably the last in the whelping,"

I developed the reasoning he outlined.

"Tiny lady, so be it,"

He carried on.

"I'm concerned about her:

I fear that she's growing weaker and weaker."

Mom left the suitcase, which she could barely carry, outside the entrance. When the meal was over, she slipped away and arranged everything in its place, as if the books too had been born on the shelves.

We were all exhausted.

Especially Grandpa.

Mom covered him with a blanket.

And we retired to bed early.

"Wake up! Wake up!"

I dreamed that I was being shaken.

"Wake up! Wake up!"

Grandpa wouldn't let go.

"Get Dad.

Horrible sobs are coming from the yard:

A puppy crying for help…"

Mom, usually a light sleeper, didn't wake up.

Dad leaped up.

Found a flashlight.

"Stay here and watch Grandpa!"

He ordered and was swallowed by darkness.

He was horrified when he returned:

The tiny lady—he found in the hole.

And brought her back to her mother.

"Sue finally drank.

And ate with gusto,"

Grandpa informed me of the good news the following day.

"With great decorum she went to move her bowels.

Passed water.

And rushed back."

With twinkling eyes and a voice filled with emotion he told me how every so often she nurses and cleans the puppies, under the watchful gaze of Champion, "who comes and goes," as if making sure everything is in good shape.

That night, Mom also woke up to heart-stopping shrieks coming from the yard.

Once again, Dad rescued the tiny one from the hole.

"Sue—the symbol of motherhood.

The epitome of devotion.

Who is being so cruel to our little peewee…?"

Grandpa wondered in a hoarse voice.

"The pups—still can't walk on their own.

So she couldn't have made it there alone."

Mom led us a small step forward.

"And twice to the same place.

That's odd, to say the least…"

Grandpa pondered out loud.

"This is a matter of life and death. A critical issue, which must be handled with the utmost caution. Thus, Champion is going back to sleeping with you!"

Dad ruled.

I lowered my gaze toward Mom, who was zipping up Grandpa's plaid slippers.

To my astonishment, she nodded.

"He never goes anywhere near them!"

I looked up at Grandpa. And even he, who had seen him "going in and out," and who always avoided taking a stand whenever there were disagreements, and who stated that he was but a "a guest for the night…" —even he agreed with them…

Suddenly I found myself standing before a fortified front.

The trust I had always placed in them was undermined.

The confidence I always had in their judgment was shattered to bits all at once.

A sense of injustice seeped in.

Simmered.

Seethed.

Anger ignited.

Burst into flames.

Singed.

Seared.

A helplessness fueled it.

Turned it into a flamethrower.

Into molten lava.

The tongues of animosity lashed out.

Ate away at every good piece of me.

I could not look at them.

Especially at Grandpa.

I separated myself from them.

And they—the more distant they became, the smaller they became.

And the smaller they became, the blurrier they became.

Until they merged into one hostile and foreign lump.

"Once bitten, twice shy.

Once bitten, twice shy."

As far as I was concerned, Grandpa could have kept on mumbling.

I looked straight at Champion:

"Come, my Ron!

We're going to bed!"

I raised my voice, so they wouldn't be able not to hear:

"Don't pay attention to them.

Who do they think they are?!

What on earth are they thinking?!

Who even needs them?!"

Slamming the door with all my might, I then opened it quietly to let him out.

With him at my side, I instantly fell asleep.

But even when fast asleep I heard—or imagined hearing (to me it is one and the same)—the scratching of his fingernails as he made his way to the garage and back.

In the morning, they resumed their routine.

I was unable to look at them.

Especially at him.

Not even when I served him lunch.

Nor at dinner.

In order to avoid crossing their paths, I set my alarm clock. And even before Robert's crowing I went to do my morning chores.

They were already in the kitchen.

Dad was flustered:

He couldn't fall asleep at night.

So as not to disturb Mom, he was reading in the kitchen.

From the corner of his eye he saw Sue running outside.

And between her teeth, poor peewee…

Through the window he followed them, until she disappeared in the darkness.

And rushed back…

Alone…

Mom admitted that had he not seen it with her own eyes, she would have never believed it.

Grandpa also turned pale:

"For a mother… to abuse like that…

Her own offspring…

Her own flesh…

Bone of her bones…"

Dad was convinced there had to be a reasonable explanation for it.

"What time is it?" he asked when Robert crowed:

"Ah, six forty-five. It's a good time to call Doctor Yehoram, before he makes his house calls."

"He immediately knew who it was," he shared with dubious satisfaction. "He claims that Sue knows the puppy won't survive. That already in the womb her siblings were developing at her expense and pushed her to bottom in the whelping."

Against my will, my gaze crossed with Grandpa's, which widened when Dad concluded that Sue had given up on her and was abandoning her to her fate.

"You don't say!

You don't say!"

Grandpa was dumfounded:

"The wonders of nature indeed…"

Mom, who never spoke about her mother in my presence, seemed lost in thought, when wondering if by chance he recalled the name of the film about the lives of Eskimos they had seen at the time, "with Mom…"

"About…

About…

About the lives…"

Against my will I was drawn in by the wondering gaze.

"About the lives of…

Eskimos…"

He replied without batting an eyelid.

"The Savage Innocents."

As if extending a long arm into the depths of a hidden past. Rummaging through the entrails of a moldy database. And offhandedly pulled out the required information.

"Do you remember that unforgettable scene:

Boys sending a grandma adrift on an ice float…"

Her passionate voice dulled and faded:

"It's the same thing…

In a canine guise…"

She concluded in a low voice as if under duress.

"Let's not confuse the laws of nature here."

He half-implored-half-cautioned her:

"The lifecycle of the Eskimo grandma had reached its end, unlike our peewee," he said, his voice softening, "who has yet to begin living hers. She has her whole life ahead of her. La vie devant soi," he repeated, merging languages as he often did when still at his best.

"And instead of fighting for her, what does her mother do?

What does she do?

What does Sue do?

Gives up…

And rushes to bring her end closer…

And how so?!

Why?!

Thus: this is not the same old story, but rather its opposite.

And in our current context, perhaps it would be appropriate to say: opposite *pole*."

With a half-smile he cleared his throat and poured forth:

"Let me tell you, my only daughter whom I love—I have been young, and I am fortunate to now be old."

And he counted off, one by one, that he was fortunate to have had a harmonious marriage to a wife who was also a loving mother. To have raised a fine daughter. To marry her off to a "family man." To nurture a relationship with a granddaughter who is starting to resemble her in her "budding youth." To enjoy reading. To be moved by classical music. To be well regarded by his "acquaintances," who continue to seek his company. To make a honorable living, even as a pensioner. To manage an independent life without being a burden on anyone… And in his old age, to have even been granted the opportunity to follow "the magnificent seven," whose development provided him with new insights…

"And the day will come when I, too…"

He looked straight at Mom,

"Will close my eyes."

"Was that all the doctor had to say?"

When the last of the echoes died out, he redirected the conversation to the exact point from which it had been diverted.

"He claims that there is no abuse or cruelty here," Dad replied. "It's natural selection. That's how it works."

Grandpa—who spent his days and nights reading literature and poetry, philosophy and science, and who often struck me as the character in a novel I had recently read, the "autodidact" who reads all the books in the local library in alphabetical order—spoke about "natural selection and the survival of the fittest, in other words: those endowed with the most developed ability to adapt." And about "the temporary status of a confirmed theory, in other words: the kind that is, in principle, a candidate for refutation, as we were taught by our master, **Sir** Karl Popper—**a Jew, by the way**," he stressed with more than a pinch of pride. And he praised that approach, "Which is far more humble than that which presumes to discern between what is true and what is false."

As he sailed further away with his thoughts, his agitation abated. And with a hushed voice he admitted that it was beyond him how, with all the support she has from all of us… Sue has reached such an odd decision, to say the least…

"I have been young, and now I am old…

I have been young, and now I am old…" he mumbled, "yet I have never seen such a thing…

What is left for me to say but:

"Be appalled… you heavens, and shudder with great horror."

For my part, "natural selection" was, at best, the name of an Israeli band. Even without understanding, I knew one thing:

Peewee must be rescued.

And that was enough for me.

I pressed her against her mother's nipple.

She hesitated for a moment.

And then latched on.

And sucked with fervor.

I carried on and pressed her against the nipple every day.

As many times as possible a day.

One day.

Two days.

Three days.

A week.

Almost two weeks.

Over time we realized that Sue had accepted the verdict.

No less, but also no more.

From that moment on, the cries of despair ceased.

* * *

The crisis of trust led to an acute sense of alienation.

From everyone.

Especially from Grandpa.

Their unjust treatment of Champion burned within me.

Blazed.

Consumed every good part of me.

A wall stood between me and them.

And it closed in on me too.

I found comfort only in the puppies, who, from one day to the next, swelled and grew a silky down:

Like tiny drunken teddy bears they stood on their feet.

Wobbled and fell.

Staggered and faltered.

And mostly developed the ability to improve their positions vis-à-vis their siblings.

When one of the plumped ones took over a nipple, the rest would storm after him, stepping on each other on the way. Pushing and trampling one another without an ounce of consideration. Certainly not toward peewee or their mother.

When one tripped, another combative brute would rush to take his place.

It was a battlefield.

An all-out war.

A hostile takeover for all intents and purposes:

Goal-driven.

Unbridled.

And devoid of compassion and mercy.

"A war of all against all." More than once I heard Grandpa exclaim in horror, witnessing the catastrophes and the bleats, which grew louder as the pups became stronger.

My stubbornness provided peewee with the necessary conditions for survival.

No more than that.

But also no less.

"Please, if you will, go and see," he said to me one day. "It's the coming of the Messiah. Before our very eyes the eschaton is taking shape, as it is written: 'The wolf will dwell with the lamb.' Though everything is still weary, seek and ye shall find. Fortunately, peewee doesn't speak veterinarian. And live she shall!" he announced excitedly.

I did not answer him.

I was incapable.

As far as I was concerned they did not exist.

Especially not him.

Nor did I make a sound when I saw Sue clenching peewee's nape in her teeth, and bolting from the garage to the kitchen.

Settling at the foot of the armchair.

And withdrawing into her breastfeeding.

Once in a sated stupor, she fell into a deep sleep, the hunched-over Sue scurried out to bring in another pup.

And devoted herself to him, too.

One by one she tended to them. The others, who were used to feeling satiated, remained awake.

In a matter of mere nights, what was meant to be quality time also turned into an all-out war between the pups, albeit slightly less fierce.

From that night on she devoted herself first to peewee:

Every night, without exception, she would bring her in first.

Clean her.

Nurse her.

When she suffered from constipation or didn't urinate enough, she would stimulate their function by licking them.

Every night she would make her rounds exactly seven times. Never did she make them six or eight times.

"It's like she can count," I found myself commenting one night, mainly to see what they thought about it.

"She probably learned from you," Dad said and laughed.

Grandpa, who thought this was "an interesting issue," viewed it as a manifestation of "developed maternal instincts. Healthy instincts, nothing more."

And yet, "she never forgets even a single puppy, and never goes back even one time too many," he brought me back to the same point I had reached without him.

At the same time a new motif began to emerge: like Honi the Circle-Drawer, Champion began circling with a proud, measured strut, his fur shining, his magnificent tail perked and wagging.

On the following nights he did not expand the radius of his circles: close enough to the center of attention and as if free of deep involvement, he made his rounds.

Never carried a pup.

Never aware of what they needed.

Never watched over them as they made their first steps.

Never drew close to them or to Sue, who treated him as if he didn't exist.

And Sue, the fatter they became, the more her nape resembled a hump. Her back became concave from a congestion of milk. Her nipples drooped. Her fur lacked luster. And she began shedding bundles of it, which, to Mom's regret, whirled in every corner.

Weeks passed.

The pups grew.

And we had to close the door and let Sue regulate the pace with which she brought them in.

Only then did he start relating to them:

Reaching out a leg.

Slightly nudging them.

Laying them on their backs.

Rolling them from side to side.

Coaxing them into play and chasing them, as he had entertained himself with Sue at the time, but with one difference: he showed not even the slightest sign of jealousy toward the pups—not in our outbursts of laughter. Nor in the warmth we showered them with. Even Sue's indifference toward him, he took for granted.

In my mind this was no trivial matter, given that from the moment of the whelping—to this day it is a riddle to me whether he associated it with her heat or the mating—his interest in the seven pups lingering between his legs was, at best, limited. And instead of a groupie, there now lived a mother under his roof, who was entirely devoted to her offspring. And this, too, he took for granted.

For my part, it was an opportunity to reintroduce him to the training regimen:

Free of her tailings, he improved his performances.

At nights—although we were both exhausted, he would go to the garage.

Whom he visited there—God only knows:

Sue?!

Offspring?!

Friends?!

After school, I always found Grandpa in the same position: seated in his chair. Bent over. His right elbow perched on his knee. His chin resting on his thumb and clasped between his fingers. His glasses sloped on his nose. And his gaze spaced out and contemplative at the same time.

First, I would power-wash the garage, seeing that the bigger the pups grew the sharper the stench became. And while dragging the mop, I would listen without commenting as he updated me on the developments.

"For many weeks I have been witnessing that which is taking place here," he enthused one day.

"I find Sue to be the symbol of devotion, the epitome of maternal insight."

Now that the pups are more independent, she allows herself to go out more frequently and for longer periods. And from the barks he ascertains that she is once again playing with Champion.

When she asks, he lets her out.

And when she scratches the door, he lets her back in.

Leaving the door open—he does not dare:

"From that we had more than enough…"

"Do you mean what I think you mean…?"

At once the lava in the seemingly extinguished volcano erupted.

As if he didn't hear, he continued to praise peewee, who was developing beautifully—even if she would not reach the size of her siblings:

She is "a mini model."

"A minion."

"Petite."

And very "coquettish."

What is there to talk about?!
A captivating pup.

"She has slowly learned to stand her ground, and she no longer shies away from the others. Although she can still be easily deceived."

"…What was I talking about?" He sailed like a ship detached from its anchor.

"About Sue, the symbol of devotion, the epitome of maternal insight, and about peewee who's developing beautifully," I retraced his steps dryly.

"Well…?"

He looked at me with a lost gaze.
"W-e-l-l..."

His tongue faltered.

In his weakness he straightened his back.

Pushed his glasses up the bridge of his nose.

Removed them.

Placed them in the pocket of his shirt.

"Well..."

As if withdrawing into himself:

"When I was left by myself..."

Dipped the tips of his toes in gushing waters.

Cleared his throat weakly.

Took a deep breath.

"Well..."

As if searching for the right tone.

"Well... when I was left to raise your mother by myself..." In an open underground tunnel echoed the tender, quiet sound of the opening chord.

He closed his eyes.

Leaned over.

Fixed his hold.

Liora Barash Morgenstern

And as if to himself, began to speak about the days in which my grandmother, his Michaelinka, fell ill. And as if against his will intimated that within days… mere days… she passed away:

In her prime.

When her entire life lay ahead of her…

In the midst of a creative thrust.

And how accomplished she was …

His thumb trembled, and his head almost drooped.

He opened his eyes, in which a grief deeper than I had ever seen before was reflected.

Supporting his right arm with his left hand, he continued in an undertone:

"Without any warning.

Without a family history of illness."

His hoarse voice cracked.

In the morning everything was fine.

At noon, a slight headache that steadily worsened.

Before sunset, nausea. Vomiting on the way back from work.

Suddenly.

In the middle of the day.

A phone call from Talinka: "Mom isn't feeling very well, she wants you to hurry home."

And who knew if not he that his work as a young, independent and ambitious accountant on the fast track was of the utmost importance to his Michaela, he mumbled, and his lips quivered.

After all, she never summoned him home in the middle of work, under any circumstance—out of sheer consideration, which "by the way, character-ized her in every aspect."

"What can I say?! She even gave birth to our Talinka before sunrise."

He dropped everything.

And ran as fast as his feet could carry him.

Saw her pallor. Her gleaming eyes. Her heavy eyelids. The helplessness.

And immediately, an ambulance.

Emergency room.

"And over there, there's always a more urgent case: they have their diagnoses and their work procedures.

That's how they save lives.

And quite often, that's also how disasters occur…"

The despondent voice dimmed.

"They diagnosed: food poisoning.

Food poisoning, my foot!!!

And go argue with them."

They insert an IV.

And the blood pressure soars.

The headache grows acute.

The nausea is unbearable:

One does not need a diploma to notice it.

He calls for help.

And they stand their ground.

"Sir, if you get in our way, we will have to ask you to wait outside."

He moistens dry lips.

Wipes sweat.

Presses his hand to her forehead.

And his Michaelinka is sinking…

And once again he calls for them.

"And these doctors, interns really, what can they do?!

Tell me not to worry…"

And within hours. Mere hours. Blurred consciousness.

"T-a-a-a-l…

T-a-a-l-i-i-i-n-k-a-a…"

Her lips uttered, the blood draining from them:

"And loss of consciousness…"

His pressing, broken voice fades.

And again urges:

At once everyone starts running around his Michaelinka.

Every muscle in his face stretches:

Measuring blood pressure.

Changing devices.

Tapping on the knees.

Bending a slumped elbow.

The knee, too, is like a rag.

The neurologist is summoned.

Closes the curtain.

Pries open the eyelids.

Focuses a flashlight beam on her pupils.

Pinches.

Pricks, the soles too.

"Sir, if you would please wait outside."

Grandpa's voice, repeating after the doctor, pierces me.

The wide door is burst open.

An orderly pushes a bed.

The IV sways.

The doctor runs.

Ventilates.

Where are they going?

X-ray.

Of the brain.

The bed squeaks.

The corridors are endless.

The elevator goes down.

Running.

Above the door, a red light cautions.

There is a line.

The door opens.

The doctor lingers.

Comes out with an analyzed X-ray:

"Massive brain hemorrhage."

Grandpa turns pale.

His veins swell.

In the neck.

In the temples.

Criss-crossing his hands as well.

Every blood cell is crying out inside him.

Back to the emergency room.

Immediately rushed to the neurosurgery department: to a big hall, to "a type of emergency unit, which nowadays exists in every department," he whispers.

Respirator. Oxygen tank. IV. Catheter. Adjusting. And again changing. Checking blood pressure. EKG. Zigzagging graph. Up. Down. They list values, of what, god knows…

The head is turned. The silky brown hair—oh, how fresh it smelled—braided warp and weft. The tongue is pulled out. In the nose—a cannula. In the throat—a feeding tube. Expectorants. Drawing phlegm.

The cold compresses on the forehead warm up in seconds. They change them. A ventilator is also brought in to help bring down the temperature.

The blood pressure spikes.

Again they prick. Draw blood: abnormal oxygen levels.

They inject. Jot down. Turn from side to side. And supine on the back.

Edema in the fingers. Spreads to the hands. The feet. The lips. The eyes. Everything is swollen.

And as the hours go by the face becomes more yellow and velvety.

The experts conduct consultations:

"Aneurysm."

"It's not an aneurysm."

I get it even without understanding.

They deliberate:

It doesn't look good.

It looks bad.

"Critical condition." They are of one mind.

We must intervene.

We mustn't intervene.

"We must let nature run its course."

The tension intensifies:

"No improvement."

We must examine further:

"X-ray with contrast material."

Portable oxygen tank.

Manual resuscitation bag.

The blood transfusion is trickling.

The IV is dripping.

Grandpa runs with the orderly.

The elevator goes down.

Everything screeches.

Another test.

And back to the department.

"Excuse me, perhaps the results have arrived?" he asks with pleading eyes.

"Just imagine: even on the brink of the abyss you must entreat them," he pours his heart out:

"Everything is ego with those doctors, you wouldn't believe it. The awe and reverence that we, the patients, treat them with, has also contributed to that," he says, and his anxious smile sours.

"Yes, they arrived:

No change."

Well, that too is for the best, he consoles himself with dimmed eyes: his Michaelinka is a tough cookie. His wife wants to live. She has whom to live for. She has what to live for…

"The condition is still critical," Grandpa reports from the department:

"A precise diagnosis, there is none, quite literally."

Unfortunately, imaging technology, or god knows what, was still in its infancy. And the doctors, too, fumbled in the dark:

"There was no C.T.

And we could not have even dreamed about an M.R.I."

Helplessness speaks from within him. Even today, when needed, the expensive machinery exists… but in a different hospital…

"Yes, hospitals have an ego, too. Imagine such an absurdity: politics even on one's sick-bed…"
Grandpa did everything within his power.

"Discretely" held consultations: doctors are also human beings. They, too, can make mistakes. And they, too, must be watched.

"**Never trust anybody but yourself**", he commands me.

The neurosurgeon at Hadassah Hospital in Jerusalem has a different approach:

"We might want to consider drainage. Otherwise…"

Suggests a consultation.

Grandpa conducts himself diplomatically.

The doctors are reluctant:

"Without trust, it's difficult to function."

And they, too, are right.

Eventually they give their consent.

The professor from Jerusalem wraps up a long day of surgeries. And toward evening he walks in refreshed.

"How do they do it, the doctors?!" he wonders.

The head of the department welcomes him.

Grandpa paces the corridor.

The consultation drags on.

And he can hardly take the tension…

Finally, the head of the department, in a white coat and the professor in a suit, tie and slight bow of the head, pass by him ceremoniously. The professor nods hello. To the head of the department, Grandpa is invisible. And as one person they are swallowed into his office, at the entrance of the department.
Fear of the boss stresses out the secretary, who urges him into the room.

The professor, proficient in departmental conduct, lets the head of the department have his say, then continues:

"Mrs. Shavit," he says, addressing the patient before the illness, "has an aneurysm: due to a convoluted fold, probably congenital, the artery wall weakens, until it ruptures. In your wife's case, a major blood vessel in the brainstem was damaged."

Removing a skull model from the shelf, he demonstrates step-by-step what happened.

Drainage can be performed.

"However, in her condition, it is inadvisable to move Mrs. Michaela to Jerusalem," he says, allowing himself a further degree of familiarity.

"First, we must do everything to lower her blood pressure. Otherwise, once I open," he continues, pointing at the location, "the blood will erupt as if from a fountain. And I won't be able to see what's going on, inside, in the skull."

I, too, shudder at hearing this "naturalistic" style, as he refers to it.

The professor is putting himself at the disposal of the head of the department, and of Grandpa.

And leaves.

In those days they were strict about visiting hours.

Him—they could not drive out.

Grandpa returned to his wife's bedside.

"Wait on the other side of the door!"

The nurse instructs.

The resuscitation team charges in.

I, too, must know:

Who?

What?

The doctor comes out:

"Shut the door!"

And once again they let him in:

"No change in her condition."

The same familiar gestures. Perhaps slightly more freedom of movement.

"It will be fine," I wish along with him.

Grandpa brings over a gramophone and records from home. In the pre-miniaturization era everything was big and cumbersome and heavy. In the corridor he sterilizes everything with cotton balls and alcohol, even the grooves of the records.

The doctors summon the head of the department:

"In her condition—this is not what your wife needs."

And to the staff's astonishment, the head of the department does not stand his ground.

In the alienated space, Andrés Segovia, whom his wife so loves, strokes emotion and tenderness on the strings of the classical guitar, and makes his way through the labyrinth of notes in the subtle theme of Bach's Chaconne.

Holding his breath, Grandpa studies her face:

A reaction—there is none.

The machinery pants and cautions.

The nurse injects.

Pumps.

Writes down.

"On the brink of the abyss—the treatment is second to none in its devotion," he says, a smile sours on his face.

"No wonder!

When in a state of unconsciousness," he snickers bitterly, "the sickness is being treated, not the patient…"

In the shortening breaks between treatments, he lets Segovia perform variations on a theme by Mozart.

And…

…As if nothing.

His heart sinks with the large hand of the white clock on the wall.

And every minute, an eternity.

And he longs for the magical touch of the 'Bachianas Brasileiras' by Villa-Lobos, who, according to his wife, merges the style of Bach with lively Brazilian music.

"And…

And…

…Not even a blink."

He prays.

Takes moonstruck oaths.

And vows never to break them.

Even hides talismans under the mattress.

And puts his trust in the second movement of Joaquín Rodrigo's 'Concierto de Aranjuez' in the restrained yet powerful performance of Julian Bream, the British musician, who moved his wife with the virtuosity of his playing and his sensitivity to nuances. "And…

Nothing."

The music plays.

And the respirator inhales and exhales:

"What a surreal vision…"

And in his heart, love. Faith. Hope.

The doctor is in the "unit."

"Any improvement?" The tone is businesslike and the gaze is yearning.

"We managed to slightly lower her temperature. To stabilize her blood pressure. It's possible there might be a bit more freedom in her movements. Her condition could change any minute. As long as the blood vessel still isn't functioning, there's no way of knowing."

"When…?"

"It varies. Usually, within ten days to two weeks from the day of the episode."

And the "sympathetic" doctor suggests trying to stimulate a response:

"Michaelinka, I'm squeezing your hand.

If you feel it, squeeze my hand back…

Just once…" he begs for his life.

For the god-knows-how-many times, he tells his wife that she wasn't feeling well and has been hospitalized. He sends her warm kisses and get well soon wishes from Talinka, who is eagerly awaiting her recovery and swift return home.

And in the meantime, until she recovers, he is here.

With her.

Not budging from her bed.

"Please, Michaelinka: one squeeze, just one."

"That's it!!!"

He turns pale:

"There's a response."

"A response, reflex—it isn't conclusive. Let her be for now. Try again later…" The doctor peeks over his shoulder.

I count the days with him:

A week has passed.

Eight days.

"In the bat of an eye," nine.

One day for each of Talinka's years, "the apple of her eye."

His eyes sink deeper into their sockets.

The tremor in his lips becomes stronger:

Oh, the relationship they have had…

The roaring laughter…

What joie de vivre. What joy of life." Longing mixes with grief and the intensity is uncontainable.

His face darkens:

On the ninth day, before sunrise, commotion.

Doctors.

Nurses.

No entry. We have an urgent case on our hands.

"How is Michaela Shavit?"

I am anxious with him.

"Not now.

Not here.

Please wait outside."

Hastened steps. Averted gazes.

His heart foresees foreboding.

I pace the hallway with him.

Time stands still.

And does not stop running out.

The hours go by:

One hour.

Two.

The doctors—evaporated.

Dropped out of sight.

The social worker—nowhere to be found.

Only nurses.

The spark of hope is fading.

His face turns even paler.

And there is no one to talk to.

Two doctors appear.

Unfamiliar faces.

Out of nowhere a senior physician emerges.

The three pass him by immersed in lively chatter, and are swallowed into the gaping mouth of the department.

The senior doctor returns.

Invites him to his office:

"Recurrent hemorrhage…

Multiple system failure…

Clinical death…"

Grandpa's eyes are torn open.

He hears and nothing sinks in.

And the doctor is in a rush.

And he disappears off the face of the department.

Grandpa shuffles his feet.

Once again puts on a sterile coat.

Covers his nose and mouth.

The red fluid pours out.

Scrubs his hands.
Same bed.

Same Michaelinka.

He strokes her.

Her forehead is warm.

Her cheek, too.

Her hand.

And her toes.

Grandpa says goodbye. And he is unable to part.

He parts. And doesn't believe he is parting.

And time stands still:

Grandpa is there.

And I am there with him.

Time goes by.

Grandpa, who refuses to be consoled, sinks into his loss:

As long as he aches for her, his Michaelinka is not dead.

To ache less is to part with her more. He does not stop hurting.

To mourn less is to lose more. He lives the tragedy every moment.

"And our Talinka is still tiny.

A little girl.

Merely nine…"

Deeper the sadness seeps in.

"It isn't fair that I had a mom only for nine years…"

His voice becomes childlike and his face contorts in horror.

"And what do you say to a nine-year-old child who loses her mother?

What is there to say at all…?"

"Mom… was exactly my age now…"

Suddenly I realize.

Grandpa does not respond:

He is with an orphaned child, whose needs he had never been aware of.

Never cooked for her. Never even fried an egg.

Never bought a thing, not even a pin or a shoelace.

Never participated in a parent-teacher conference.

Never accompanied her to a doctor's appointment.

He is petrified.
Everything threatens him.

Worst of all…
The emptiness in the mornings…

To detach himself from the bed was as hard as parting the Red Sea.

To send the child to school was a preternatural effort.

Apart from Talinka, everything was redundant:

The day.

The night.

Food.

Drink.

He couldn't swallow a thing.

He was redundant.

And there is no helping hand, a voice from the grave utters from within him.

I, an expert on Sue's genealogy many generations back, was acquainted for the first time with his parents, Matty and Rivka, who, when "what happened, happened"—were not in good health. And with my grandmother's parents, Loneck and Bronia, who were saved from the Holocaust but not from the nightmares.

"What is there to say?!" He suppressed a moan.

"Everything is water under the bridge, everything is water under the bridge," he repeated as if ignoring an ache:

"What happened, happened…

And life must go on."

Slowly slowly he began doing things his own way, to the best of his ability, which was infinitely inferior to his wife's:

"And who could compare to her and her mental strengths.

Always attentive.

And what a sense of humor…"

Another wave of longing washed over him.

"Her capacity for containment was a sound box, compared to which even a Stradivarius is but a cricket."

But he was young, "inexperienced."

And his life rotated around one axis:

Work.

There was nothing left for him but to hope his Michaelinka knew how much he loved her.

How much he loves her…

His eyelids drooped.

Only the puppies' barks rasped from time to time.

I, who was beside myself, rolled up the hose.

I put the mop back, too.

"Ellienka," he said, finally opening his eyes and staring at me. "Why am I telling you all this?!"

As if the valve of a pressure cooker popped. And once the gases of life regulated, it sealed, never to be reopened.

"…What was I talking about?" he looked at me with glazed eyes.

"About Sue, who's a symbol of devotion and motherhood…" I repeated, until eventually the threads of his tangled thoughts raveled. And in an exhausted voice he began talking again about the needles the insatiable pups stick in her nipples. And about the pain he reads on Sue's face. And as if mumbling to himself, the more he contemplates motherhood… the more he is pushed into the corner with respect to fatherhood…

"Seven pups he sired, and I doubt he even knows he is a father.

Tell me, Ellienka, with complete honesty:

What is Champion doing?

How is he contributing?

What is he giving of himself to the pups…?

He stood on the bridge he built between two peaks, and looked down at Champion.

"If he didn't live at home," I replied, the flickering ember inside me sparked again, "trust in him that he would know exactly what to do. Here, with us, it's just unnecessary:

So what does it say?

That he doesn't know he's a father?

That he doesn't know how to be a father?

That he isn't a good father?

That he's a no-good father?

That he doesn't care about them?

Why?"

"That's a fascinating observation." He was caught by the horns in the thicket of his thoughts: "It has far-reaching implications… An entire worldview is hiding behind it…"

He shifted his supporting right hand. Dropped his left. Fumbled through the pocket of his shirt. Fished out his glasses. Put them on. Pressed them against the bridge of his nose. Looked up. And fixed his gaze on me:

"With your permission, Ellienka, I have another small question for you." He cleared his throat. "Well:

if his family members live in conditions that are more or less acceptable," he asked with an ambivalent voice, "is that enough for you to consider him a good father… or… perhaps… that is not quite the case?"

If the pups are fine. And Sue doesn't have a problem. And he—even though you separated him from his family—checks what's going on in the garage each and every night, that means that in his own way he's looking out for them. And without sparing him I threw in his face that I don't forgive any of them—especially not **him!**—who followed Champion and saw how he treats them.

"So if **for him** that's fatherhood, **so what?!**

So that's just the way it is."

Once the stinger of the indignation was removed, the animosity that was consuming me began to withdraw. The walls that had been closing in on me, came tumbling down. And as the distance I kept from myself grew shorter, everything began to take on its former dimensions and colors.

"This is a truly Kafkaesque allegation," he debated with himself:

"Joseph K also found himself wrongfully accused one day. And what was he guilty of? What was he guilty of?" he kept repeating. "Existence. Sheer existence. Existence, as such. There is a reason that from the very beginning the legal authority is woven warp and weft in his daily routine: at home. At work. Wherever he turns, there lies his guilt. And since we are dealing with existential guilt, the choice is reduced to one of two: either 'ostensible acquittal' or 'indefinite postponement.' '*Uma qa mashma lan?*' he asked me in Aramaic, 'and what does it mean to us?' he translated. The perpetuation of guilt. "And yet, as long as breath is in him, hope is not gone. And the evidence is that when he is about to be executed, and 'a window opened out, somebody, made weak and thin by the height and the distance, leant suddenly far out from it and stretched his arms out even further…' Joseph K wondered: 'Would anyone help?!' and parts with the world 'like a dog!'

"Hence, there are two sides to the coin," he said, as if deliberating with himself. "Oh, well. Justice is on your side: nothing can be derived from this about Champion. And "*leit man de'falig*", he switched again to Aramaic, "and no one can dispute", he translated: "our dog was entitled to a 'definite acquittal.' "

* * *

At the time, as far as I was concerned, Grandpa could have kept debating with himself in Aramaic or any other language, and he could have heaped his literary references on me as much as his heart desired.

Now, when what connects me to him is the very same thing that had separated me from him back then, and

I am no longer tripping between scales, I struggle to contain the accelerating intensity and overwhelming force.

And absentmindedly my attention is drawn to a package containing four records, which Mom had discovered behind his volumes of the Encyclopedia Hebraica (which were the tallest in his library) while clearing his apartment to rent out; so she told me on my twenty-first birthday. And she also handed me the note Grandpa had attached to it.

And I, who if not for the records, wouldn't remember a single oeuvre that Grandpa played for his Michaelinka, recite to myself:

> To Ellienka,
>
> Today, as you turn one year old,
> I have wrapped this package in fine gift wrap,
> For you to open on your twenty-first birthday.
>
> This is not just another gift.
> It is unique of its kind.
>
> From a grandfather, who even when he wanders far,
> Wishes that one day,
> You and your mother will find adequate mental space,
> To allow its strings to play in the depths of your souls.
>
> Your loving Grandpa
> 1.11.1981

Two well-balanced voices echo now within me at the same time:

"Adequate mental space"—vibrates the yearning intonation.

"The episode… What happened, happened…"—voices from the grave reply within me.

Absentmindedly, my hand drops to the side of the bed.

Sue raises her head.

I pat it.

And with an ever-present ambivalence I wonder, how is it that despite the oppression that was her fate, as long as he was alive, she never stopped clinging to Champion. And when he suffered a massive cerebral hemorrhage, was taken to the vet, and never came back—for an entire week she would not eat even a crumb. And for months she would cry out to him in Wolfish:

"Aoouu.

Aoou."

And even as the gaps between the heart-wrenching cries grew further apart, she would not stop sniffing for his traces in every corner.

And I ponder the youngest pup, Josh, who, as long as Champion was alive, could not understand why he deserved everything first. And yet it was he who came to greet us when we returned empty-handed from Doctor Yehoram.

Crawled into the corner.

And did not move:

A day.

Two days.

Three.

Almost seven.

And then, uncharacteristically, he would race each evening to the gate and bark for hours.

God knows to whom:

A father? A sibling? A friend?

Everything hangs heavy.

Everything is burdensome.

Even the darkness.

I take off the blanket.

And get up.

Approach the copper lamp in the corner.

And turn on the light.

Retrace my steps.

About to get back in bed.

And in the yellowing light cast by the frayed parchment lampshade, staring at me from the linen chest is 'The Little Prince,' who has "hair that is the color of gold." And in my heart play the poetic words of Grandpa, who, in his fine calligraphy, dedicated a copy of the book to me which he had bound in leather, with the figure of the Little Prince engraved in gold:

> To Ellienka, my granddaughter,
>
> my one and only, whom I love,

> From Grandpa,
>
> A grown up who grew old,
>
> Who thanks to you is reminded
>
> That "An old sight too has its moment of birth."
>
> And that he, too, was once a child.
>
> And that at nights, loves "to listen to the stars."

> Passover Seder, 1989

"I am entrusting you with a loyal friend who will accompany you wherever you go." Echoing in open channels inside me, his tone moist with emotion, as he gave it to me in exchange for the Afikoman in the last Seder he presided over. "From different perspectives in time and space, in 'The path still stretching on, long and wide'—you will yet see its landscapes and learn that they are ever widening and deepening," he added in his flowery manner, which at the time brought a smile to my face.

I—who in every state of mind read his words anew, and who's always enchanted by the beauty of his writing and by the simplicity and the wisdom of understanding what is truly important in life; who, every time I read him, find a different metaphor unfolding before me; who has no doubt that 'The Little Prince' is one of the three books I would take to a deserted island (I'm still undecided about the others)—am amazed by how the Little Prince understood the way one must treat a "bad seed…" That "one must destroy it as soon as possible, the very first instant that one recognizes it." Otherwise, it is something "you will never, never be able to get rid of…" And how one must handle "volcanoes…" which, "if they are well cleaned out, burn slowly and steadily, without any eruptions." And therefore, even the "extinct" ones must be cleaned out, too, because "One never knows!"

And from the volcanoes within me, my thoughts wander to Adi (a lawyer nowadays), who also considers 'The Little Prince' as her "book of books," and who often laughs with more than a shred of cynicism, that when Saint-Exupéry wrote "Straight ahead, you can't go very far…" he must have been thinking about her and her colleagues in the profession.

With pangs of conscience and heavy-hearted, from the stage I once again swing my baton toward Grandpa, who, once the conversation died down, shoveled food into his mouth, wiped his lips with a napkin and with great effort dragged his feet towards his afternoon nap, which seemed more necessary than ever. Even to cover himself—he did not have enough strength.

I kissed his forehead.

His eyes betrayed an outburst of emotions, above which new contemplations hovered.

I left the door to my room open as well.

Apart from the crackling of coal in the burning fireplace in the living room, and the austere light cast by the halogen lamp upon my books and notebooks scattered around me to no avail—the house was pitch black and completely silent.

The hour grew late.

The rain poured down.

And Grandpa did not wake up…

Before the key rattled in the lock, Champion burst out of Grandpa's room.

"Yes, I love you too.

What a heartwarming welcoming."

Mom replied to being leaped at.

"What do you have to say about my shopping spree?!"

She laughed and said that she had meant to buy only a cinnamon cake and dry food, which the pups devoured as if a battalion of soldiers lived here, and ended up emptying out the aisles.

Before changing into dry clothes, she went out to pick lemon verbena, lemon balm, melissa, sage, lemongrass and a bunch of freesia. Gathering her silky brown hair into a ponytail, she rushed down in her white high collar tracksuit, which flattered her figure and accentuated her exotic skin tone and brown almond eyes.

"Such displays of affection—I lately receive only from Champion…" She laughed when I hugged her, and wondered if there was a power outage in the house:

"Because the neighbors' houses are glowing brightly.

And here—pitch blackness."

With my stomach in knots, I explained that Grandpa was sleeping.

And I had homework to do.

"Until he wakes up, I'll put away the groceries, brew some nice herbal tea, and for once we'll sit together in leisure."

The knot in my stomach loosened only when Grandpa shuffled toward us, struggling to tie the belt of the new wool robe Mom had bought him.

"A little birdy whispered in my ear that you had a good rest."

With a smile she expelled the "depressing gloom." The soft light spread by the plaster lamps attached to the walls and the whispering embers and the breaths she blew onto the logs she added, filled the atmosphere with intimacy and festivity.

"Mom is home, light prevails…

Mom is home, light prevails…"

Grandpa reiterated softly, and it seemed to me as though he wasn't necessarily referring to my Mom.

I helped him sit down in the armchair, facing the burning fire. Champion, slouching at his feet, didn't bother to get up even when I rolled in the laden tea cart.

Mom spread out a white lace tablecloth and set the table for Dad as well. She arranged the bouquet of white and purple freesia, and in between placed yellow ones, which emanated a pleasant scent; setting the vase in the center, she pulled the table toward Grandpa.

"Good thing you bought dry food for the pups," I raised a conversation topic. "Because just today

137

Grandpa told me that nursing has become a night-mare for Sue."

Mom preferred drinking her tea while it was still boiling hot:

"Afternoon tea like in the old days, remember?"

Seemingly half floating and half flooded, he sipped and did not utter a word.

Champion burst out running, crossing the patio separating the entrance and the guest room, in which, to this day, under a ceiling of glass bricks, tall bamboo canes grow with narrow, long leaves, tropical flora entwined between them.

Even though the patio is off limits for the dogs, Dad didn't reprimand him.

He even took the mud streaked across his bright shirt in good spirits.

When Dad took his place to Mom's right, she eventually started talking:

"Your ninth birthday,

Ellienka, is approaching.

Every birthday is worth celebrating.

But this year… especially…"

She intonated while patting her knee.

"W-hy **es**-pe-**cia**lly…?"

The accentuations fidgeted.

With a hoarse, exhausted voice, Grandpa thanked her for the tea, which "hit the spot."

And apologized for being "slightly fatigued."

And with our permission, he will retire to read.

"What's wrong?

Should I call the doctor?

Actually, why am I asking?

I'll order a house call—and that's that!"

Champion, who had resumed his slouching position at Grandpa's feet, shook himself and remained with perked ears, shifting his head from side to side.

"Talinka, please, I insist:

What's the matter with you…?!"

With a hoarse voice he called her to order.

And wondered, since when is an old man not allowed to be slightly tired:

He idled around all day.

"And there is nothing more exhausting than doing nothing."

Unless the doctor wants to read his book for him, he softened with a stroke of humor.

Champion shook himself again.

And resumed his slouch.

He reminded Mom, who wrung her hands, that he is used to doing whatever he feels like, whenever he feels like it. And if he wishes to rest for a bit, he does not find that this requires "medical approval."

When she remarked that he had been alone all day, he clarified to her that apart from when he rested, he had not had a single moment to himself:

In the morning he was with the pups, and with Sue and Champion, who, at the mention of his name, pricked up an ear. Upon my return he talked with me. "And many significant things… I am learning from my granddaughter…"

And in such wintry weather, there is nothing more enjoyable than curling up under a blanket and reading a book:

"What's the big deal?!

What's wrong with that?!

Unless you insist that in order to do so I must bring you a doctor's note."

And with more effort than usual, he wrested himself out of the armchair.

"No!"

He stopped her when she rushed toward him.

"I'm asking you: let me manage on my own."

He barely dragged his feet.

And Champion accompanied him.

Mom picked up crumbs. Straightened out her tight tracksuit. Gathered stray strands into her ponytail. And apologized for not being in the mood right now for anything.

"And anyway, there's still time."

We served him dinner in bed.

Grandpa ate "not too bad."

To get up—he did not have the strength.

The following day, it was as if he had sunk deeper.

On the third day, despite his objection, she arranged a house call. Dr. Berger, the family physician, had heard much about him and was glad to finally meet him.

The examination revealed nothing new:

"Rest. Rest.

And once again, rest," he instructed.

Before washing his hands, he prescribed him geriatric vitamins for strengthening his constitution, which is recommended for anyone his age. When he came back to take his bag, Mom was waiting for him in her coat.

"Mrs. Yovel," he offered gallantly, "if you must go out in this weather, please let me escort you."

Dad implored her to give him the prescription, but she had other errands and left with the doctor.

She returned from the on-duty pharmacy in Netanya pale:

"I am not at my best," she explained.

She had "just a tiny bit" of a headache. She felt "slightly" nauseous. She was "somewhat dizzy." And suspected that she, too, was "starting to come down with some kind of flu."

In the morning she woke up early to close the shutters tighter.

I was about to enter the kitchen when her agitated voice emerged from the other side of the closed door.

I quietly set down my backpack: I knew about the "weakness in the legs," but I had no idea that Grandpa also suffered from "weakness of the elbows and floating joints. And then I… break out in cold sweat…" At first, I didn't get it. "My pulse… is racing. My mouth as dry as clay. And my head becomes empty and spins…"

The earth shook under my feet.

My knees weakened.

My mouth dried up like clay.

And my heart skipped a beat.

At school many of the students and quite a few teachers were also absent. It was not the flu that worried me, but rather the symptoms…

I had to know:

What was wrong with her, with Mom.

I had no patience to hear from Dad again about Grandpa's condition. Nor was I interested in hearing that my birthday was also affecting her. And I had enough of him going on about "repression" and the "price" Mom was paying for it.

"When have you become an expert on that, too?!" she wondered.

And she was outraged when he asked her that for once she let him say what he felt: with all his criticism against her, and not from today… in the matter of equal rights and responsibilities at home, he never had any reservations.

"Why shouldn't you allow yourself mental support:

Today there's no longer any shame in it," he implored her.

"**Shame**?!

Today there's **no longer any shame in it?!**

And when was there shame in it?!"

My concern was corrosive.

My impatience grew.

Suddenly, out of nowhere, demons appeared, which distressed her night after night, demons that Dad was also familiar with… And Mom had no intention of allowing them to wreak havoc upon her during the days as well.

As if that wasn't enough, a golem showed up as well, and Dad was convinced that it would rise against her, unless Mom received mental support, which would help her create the conditions to allow the demons to return to the bottle. In the hope that finally, once and for all, she would manage to put back the cork and seal it properly.

And Mom rushed to reclaim them.

And asked him to let her handle them on her own.

Silence panted on the other side of the door.

And the anxiety—in my heart.

With no other choice, I hauled my bag onto my shoulder.

"Talinka," he addressed her softly, "when Dad isn't feeling well, you order a house call even if it's against his will. Right?"

"Tell me: **right or wrong?**" he insisted.

"What is this, kindergarten?" she replied and smirked.

"**Right or wrong?**" He stood his ground. And asked that she take notice of how difficult it is to get an answer out of her to the simplest of questions.

"True, Professor Yovel," she replied with a childish tone.

"So you're not advocating the policy of an ostrich?" He would not let go.

"There is some truth in your argumentation, my educated colleague," she said sneeringly.

"Then why do you expect me to bury my head in the sand?!"

Half triumphant and half wrangling he reminded her that when Shlomo Zehavi was having a crisis, she was the one who convinced him to turn to therapy:

"Practice what you preach," he served her an outstanding check.

I heard or imagined I heard (to me it is one and the same) her rubbing her hands together and asking him to tell her "with complete honesty" what good it did Shlomo, who was still unable to develop a relationship with a woman:

"Big deal! Big goddamn deal!"

And she recommended that next time he spare her such dubious examples, which accomplish the exact opposite.

"This is about you. You owe it first and foremost to yourself. It can't go on this way… I, at least, won't…"

I sat down.

The cool floor burned under me.

I took off my backpack.

Put it down quietly.

And my breath caught in my chest when he began talking about the family history and the tests she had undergone:

"C.T…"

M.R.I…"

And the results…

All

Confirm:

"Everything

…is in order."

I could barely stifle my sigh of relief.

Apart from that, I didn't care about anything: not whether Mom believed I would accept that this year my birthday was "especially worth celebrating…" and not about the fact that she did not open her heart to him only to have him "play on her guilt with the virtuosity of a master."

Mom was silent.

And so was Dad.

I also wasn't bothered by the time that passed, until I heard her mumbling with a somewhat reconciled voice:

"I am a strange combination of a mixer and a cemented cistern which does not lose a drop, as Rabbi Eliezer ben Horkenus's retentive mind was described: everything gets mixed inside me and nothing is ever lost. And you're an incorrigible fixer: you want to fix a problem and move on, as if it never existed…"

From my current metaphorical outlook, as I am in the midst of writing my doctoral dissertation, I cannot help but take notice of Mom's methodical way of using this linguistic means: as with every metaphor, Mom creates a paradoxical collision. Since it is outright self-evident that Mom is neither "a mixer" nor a "plastered cistern," just as Dad is not an "incorrigible fixer," these paradoxical collisions allow her to create metaphorical spacing. And in turn, the metaphorical spacing provides her with optimal distance that enables her to clarify in which sense is she talking about "a mixer and a plastered cistern" and an "incorrigible fixer," rather than about her and Dad. Thus, this means of linguistic usage allows her to express, with utmost precision, what she intends to say, without provoking any unnecessary objection.

Only that all this was light years away from me when I stood up.

Massaged my frozen buttocks.

"I can only conclude from this that you've given up on my anxieties," her voice became wistful: "Otherwise, you, who look down on psychology, wouldn't wash your hands of this and refer me to therapy."

Dad asked her not to put words in his mouth and not use every word he uttered against him, because nothing good would come out of it…

"Ido, let's not open up a new front: Ellienka will be late. And you also have to get to the office," she said, redirecting the morning back to its course.

And with a low voice added that she longs for the day when he will listen and simply say:

"I heard.

I understand.

Without giving advice.

Not every talk calls for action."

Slowly slowly the storm blew over.

I reslung my backpack on my shoulder.

Retraced my steps on my tiptoes.

And decisively advanced toward the door.

Champion and Grandpa walked in after me. The lucidness of his gaze and the color of his cheeks attested to an improvement in his condition. Mom, whose stomach, like most thin people, becomes blocked when she's stressed, also nibbled on something. And just in case, remained home with Grandpa for another day.

The following day she returned to work, and Sue greeted me at the gate. At the entrance she turned her tail on me and vanished into thin air, as if compensating for the period in which she was bound to the pups. Champion, who raced to get there first, went back to lying at my feet during mealtimes, eagerly awaiting his treats.

The dinner table conversations once again revolved around current affairs in Israel and around the globe, mainly for the sake of Grandpa, who had weaned himself from the different media outlets "which are competing with each other to incite their readers."

"Let's not kid ourselves," I often heard him say:

"Style is message par excellence.

And I will not be a party to it."

I took pleasure in the loftiness of the conversation, from Dad who spoke about the "euphoria" that took hold of us following our swift triumph in the Six Day War, to Mom who concurred with Dad, a victory of the likes we had not experienced since David defeated Goliath.

"Enlightened occupation is a contradiction in terms," she recited to me.

In one voice they spoke about the occupation, that "if they don't find a way to end it, it will turn into the First Intifada." "But not the last…" Dad cautioned. With visual language Mom illustrated "the West— smugly sitting by the 'fleshpots' while neglecting vital interests. And the leaders of Islamic fundamentalism—who, with Oriental patience, are lurking for an opportunity." Dad once again warned that "if the West doesn't act quickly to unite the moderate forces that exist in the Arab world as well, terrorism will spread like wildfire. No country will be immune." And at that point in time, he still pinned his hopes on the conversations that were to take place between the leaders of the two "superpowers." Like him, Mom also believed in the emerging prospects of ending the "Cold War," and even back then predicted that it would bear implications for the chances to settle the conflict in our region.

Among other topics, the issue of the anticipated wave of immigration from the former Soviet Union was also raised at the table. And Dad predicted that it would "reshuffle—though not for long!—the demographic deck held by the Palestinians." Apart from "injecting new blood of educated immigrants," they were both wishing for an enlightened leadership that would know how to take advantage of the narrow window of opportunity about to open in order to increase the efforts to reach direct channels of communication:

"Zealousness, especially religious," they agreed, "undermines moderate foundations everywhere…"

When she deliberated, as she still does, over how to enable the new immigrants to become acquainted with the reality of life here before they drop their ballot into the box, he raised the possibility (which he still doesn't rule out): of introducing a third amendment to the Law of Return and to enact a naturalization process (like they do in the States, for example), "so that they will vote for what's best for them here, rather than against what they left behind," as he explained to Grandpa, who nodded.

The moment he touched upon the increase in suicides among soldiers—Mom pierced him with a look that took the wind out of the sails of the conversation.

"The change in the menu is to the pups' liking," Grandpa broke the silence. "And despite this, they will not stop harassing her:

Sue runs for her life.

And they don't give up.

If they are mature enough to chase the nipple, they are mature enough to settle for solid food," he said, sounding more determined than ever.

By the way, Mom suggested that before we allow them to enter the kitchen, we let them eat solid food in the garage.

Grandpa was pleased.

So was Dad.

In this pleasant atmosphere Dad raised a new subject: We all love the magnificent seven. But after all, we already have two dogs. And the pups will soon be weaned. And we should start thinking about finding them proper homes:

"**We're not talking** about..." he stressed and paused, "tomorrow morning…" he looked up at Mom.

And not about the day after tomorrow…

But we have to start preparing ourselves to part from them.

Mom lowered her head.

And twiddled a ball of Sue's fur between her fingers.

"Apropos of Sue," Grandpa carried on the conversation, saying that during the days he spent in bed regaining his strength, he had time to think: in the history of philosophy it was not the famous duo, Socrates, who strove to prove to his interlocutors that they did not know what they thought they knew, and Plato, his disciple, who put "his teacher's provocations into writing. But, rather, it was Aristotle—who had the audacity and integrity to praise idleness and its vital role in reaching intellectual breakthroughs." A dubious smile spread across his face.

From a distance of place and time, I am amazed at how nimbly he skipped across thousands of years, and returned to our conversation and to my "good reasoning," when I drew his attention to the injustice he had done him:

"If I spoke canine, I would apologize to you, Champion."

At the mention of his name, he rushed to Grandpa and placed his head on his thigh.

Mussing his shiny fur, Grandpa noted that while soul-searching, he had realized that not only had Champion stopped harassing Sue since the whelping, but throughout his current visit… toward him, too—he demonstrates hyper-consideration:

"You might have noticed, my Champion, that I am no longer as steady as I used to be."

And now, being exempt from competing with Sue, who has followed him devotedly from her early days, he is bestowing upon him special attention.

"And had we not talked," he addressed me.

"And had it not been for the blessed idleness," he continued, and stared at his daughter:

"I would have taken no notice of this, either."

And "avowedly" apologized for the mistreating of Champion when supporting his expulsion from the mother of his offspring and his pups.

Dad was silent.

Mom, too, didn't utter a word.

"I feel just like you," he addressed me once again: "I, too, am unable to tell whether the position I held has affected his fatherhood, but that does not mean I had the right, and certainly not the justification, to treat him as I did." And even now Champion held no grudge against him, and hadn't changed his attitude toward him in the least, on the contrary.

"Please, Ido."

With the wave of his hand he hushed Dad, lest he forgets;

At the time he justified this with the saying—

"Once bitten, twice shy…"

As if withdrawing into himself:

"I was speaking about my own scar.

Or to be precise, mine and your mother's."

He cleared his throat, and his voice remained muffled.

"When what happened, happened…" he took a deep breath:

"Your mother was indeed exactly your age, Ellienka…"

And the moisture returned to his voice when he spoke about my birthday… which for him, too, holds a special meaning: how fortunate and how blessed he is to have me as a granddaughter.

"And as for the scar…"

Once again the vitality drained:

"The scar cannot be erased.

And every now and then, it still itches…"

He spoke to me, and looked sideways at his daughter.

"However, neither a bite nor a scar can justify casting aspersions on a dog who cannot defend himself. Thus, I cannot but hope that next time I will be wise enough not to act heartlessly…"

I didn't need more than that.

If I still had an ember left inside me, it too had extinguished.

Dad brought the video camera. Mom commemorated him squinting as he took his imaginary hat off to Grandpa:

"Soon we will celebrate the bar mitzvah of our acquaintance.

And it's the first time I've heard such words from you."

He wore the imaginary hat again. And took it off to me, too. And concluded with an awkward bow accompanied by a twirling hand gesture:

"The peewee owes her life to the two of you.

And who knows better than you, Dad, what they say about he who saves one soul in Israel."

3

Now, as I stand at the front of the stage, hearing the tempos and the dynamics, and as I navigate more freely between the scales, the passion is stronger than ever.

The baton is alert.

And I long to be carried forward.

Onward.

To trace the voices and the silences, until there remains not a shred of a single cell that isn't an integral part of texture.

And once the last chord dies out…

The door opens again.

It's Josh, the youngest pup to whom Sue gave birth on a surreal patriotic Scud missile night in the midst of the first Gulf War in a shallow pit she dug in the patio.

And I recall that until I realized that it was Sue there, warming a pup, and not the black rock in the patio— even Mom did not suspect. Partly because when she became pregnant with seven, she swelled accordingly. And mostly, due to the fact that from the day we gave away the last of the puppies, upon the first sign of Sue going into heat, Mom rushed to remove Champion to the kennel. Seeing that the pup was conceived by the Holy Spirit, right then and there he was given the name: Joshua. And being a single pup to his parents, without further ado it was clear: Josh is staying.

Today, he too has grown old.

And he no longer pushes the door with force as he used to.

Sue sluggishly rises.

And slowly stumbles away.

Josh, who tyrannizes her as his father once did, as evident even now by the dreadlocks she always has on her nape, bares his teeth.

I warn him.

He does not react.

I call her.

Sue staggers.

Josh precedes her.

And lifts his head.

I pull my arm away.

Reprimand him.

And he ignores me.

Sue collapses by his side.

Sticks out her tongue.

And passionately licks his ear.

I close my eyes.

And with an odd sadness I am carried away toward Grandpa, who wasn't in the garage upon my return from school. I called out to him. And he didn't answer. Eventually I went into his room.

And I found him slouched in the rocking chair, with 'The Little Prince' resting on his knees, opened to a random page.

When his staring gaze stumbled upon me, his face lit up.

"Why are you not with the pups?"

I asked.

"Why are you not in the garage?"

I wouldn't let go.

"Can we not ever pick a different subject to talk about?!"

He finally wondered with a bleary voice.

That evening, Dad announced that the ad would be published in two local papers over the weekend. And he tasked me with rounding up the inquiries and screening the callers.

Mom sat in the armchair in the TV nook in the kitchen, and made use of the time to return phone calls she hadn't gotten around to in the office.

Champion and Sue accompanied Dad and me.

Dad barely managed to stop him from charging at the food, which the pups had devoured entirely in the blink of an eye, leaving not a single crumb.

When we let them in:

He burst forth, obviously, first.

Sue behind him.

And the trail of scurrying teddy bears was led by peewee, who rapped against the floor and hovered above it like a wind-up toy.

Sue fled as fast as her legs could carry her and took cover underneath the armchair.

Mom bent over and buried her head in her fur.

Champion noticed and rushed to nudge her and take her place.

Mom scolded him and continued to smoothen her fur, rolling the never-ending balls she had shed.

"He's bullying her.

Call him," she requested.

When he didn't react, she instructed me to call her, "And you'll soon see an abracadabra," she promised.

"Suki, come to…"

Before I could complete the sentence, he presented himself beside me.

It's an "elementary trick in reverse psychology," she explained:

With him—there are no two ways about it.

With her, it never has any effect.

Just as she avoids confrontations with the "father of her offspring," she also doesn't compete with him for attention.

Grandpa suggested a different hypothesis:

Being mature and wise, **she**… knows how to calculate her conduct.

She… is not preoccupied with nonsense.

And she avoids instigating futile confrontations.

No matter how hard we try, the other… —there is no way of changing.

I was enraged by her self-effacement and submissiveness before Champion.

"She… is acting as she acts…" Grandpa said in her defense.

"Everyone acts as they act—so does Champion!"

As if it had not been extinguished, at once the lava in the volcano inside me reignited and blazed:

"That's always true! That isn't saying anything!" I confronted him.

"Slow down there, my granddaughter," he requested. "It is indeed a truism that is by definition self-evident. But that does not mean it is easy to internalize it, let alone come to terms with it. Instead of nurturing futile expectations and suffering bitter disappointments and disillusionments, Sue… labors to constitute a solid and supportive family. And does so with unmatched success.

She bears the responsibility. And she possesses the authority. Whereas Champion renounces responsibility, and he does not have authority, either: he, as always, is first…whereas she, undisputedly, is head of the family."

And with a feeble voice he admitted that under different conditions he would have wondered how this does not provoke him to jealousy, which does not exist in Sue—"For better or worse…"

As if they were two noble horses, Dad rushed to hitch the responsibility and authority to a different wagon, which he sent on its way with a vote of confidence, trusting that I would know how to calculate my actions and to sort the dog lovers from the rest of the applicants:

"In the end we will make the decisions together. And I would like to hope, that not being alone…"

From that evening on, apart from at mealtimes, Grandpa seldom left his room.

And each day more time elapsed, until his clouded gaze slowly began to clear.

On Friday, as he leaned against Mom to sit down for breakfast, Dad called me to the phone. It was obvious to me who it was, because who other than Adi would call so early?

"I'm calling about the ad."

I was surprised by an amiable male voice.

I wrote down his phone number.

And promised to call upon my return.

In class I asked what, in Adi's opinion, was most important to the pups.

"Piece of cake:

LWS—

Love, warmth and security,

Like everyone else."

"And stability, what about that?"

"Part of security."

I thought so too.

"And support?"

"The same."

I did not see eye-to-eye with her.

"For you, SLW: with support, love and warmth, security is guaranteed."

Eventually we settled on LWSS.

"What are you going to do about those who never had a dog?"

I explained that I would find out whether they ever raised a cat, a hamster, a parrot, a silk worm, or whatever. And why this time they want to go for a dog.

"And if… if they had a dog once… and something happened to him…?" I assured her that if he was run over while chasing a dog in heat, that doesn't say anything about them.

"And what about those who want a dog to guard their house or something like that?"

I wanted them to love him regardless. And besides, to this day it isn't obvious to me that ours excel at that of all things.

For me—it was enough.

Not for Adi (who not by coincidence chose law as her profession):

"It's better if we're sure from the get-go that the entire family is really into it. Otherwise, we can get stuck with those who today feel like getting a puppy, and tomorrow will feel like getting something else instead…"

That really stressed me out.

"If anything, then where they live: an apartment is also okay, if they take them out three times a day. And if they live in a house, what happens if they damage the garden?"

I spoke quickly, so she wouldn't be able to get a word in.

"And the fact that they shed fur doesn't count?"

"And nibbling on the furniture?" she continued in the same vein.

We concluded that it was enough for now.

And if I thought of any more questions, we'd rack our brains then.

There aren't that many calls, I updated her during the week. But whoever calls has heaps and heaps of questions. Only one asked what I wanted to know about them. The rest didn't understand what I wanted from them:

Like, what?! It's **just** a puppy!"

Talking exactly like her older brother, Idan, she made me swear that I would remain "cool as a cucumber":

Not to give a hoot about anyone.

And not to back down on anything.

Fortunately, Skype did not exist at the time. And so she couldn't see how I blushed when I detailed all the trouble Champion had caused us when he was a pup:

Ripped books from cover to cover.

Ate underwear, only Mom's.

Tore holes in the drips with his teeth, and the garden was flooded.

Eventually, even my parents, who are crazy about dogs, thought about giving Champion away.

And then, completely innocently, I ask what they would have done in their place.

One, out of sheer panic, slammed the phone in my face.

In fact, it was only when Adi couldn't understand how I could have kept such a significant thing from her, that I began to realize how persuasive I am.

So she would understand what I was going through, I also told her about the woman who suddenly remembered that actually, she did have a dog once:

It was a long time ago.

For two weeks—tops.

Meaning, it doesn't count.

He barked too much, so she gave him away to the military, to the police, to an animal protection society or something like that.

"We must make sure that doesn't happen to us," she panicked.

"Especially, not with peewee…"

I blurted out.

And my heart skipped a beat.

It was clear to Adi that I was so worried about her because I had become attached to her the most after saving her.
I knew that wasn't it at all.

"She's charm on all fours," I tried.

"My Mom calls that 'rich people's problems,'" she said and laughed.

"All the others are suspicious as hell," I insisted.

"She…

Really isn't…"

Finally it hit me, and I realized what was troubling me so much about her.

The butterflies in my stomach did not fly away even when she swore on Tush Tush the Third that, manipulative and goal-oriented that I am, I would find her a great home.

On Saturday Mom woke up early to weed the garden and clear the rest of her day for Grandpa, who had spent the entire week all by himself. And she announced that she would not take any phone calls.

In the evening, while running his fingers through his hair that sprouted grey on his temples, Dad inquired about my progress.

Grandpa yawned.

Mom looked exhausted as well.

And I really didn't feel like talking.
"It'll take some time," I said in brief.

I told them only about one family—Yehuda and Ruthie, and their four children, Jonathan, Yalli, Gilya and Raphael—who were interested in what I wanted to know about them.

"No one is standing with a stopwatch in his hand," Dad assured me, and told me they should come on Saturday.

* * *

Throughout the week, the moment I inserted the key in the front lock, Champion would push the door open and burst out running toward Grandpa, who had become increasingly listless the longer he stayed away from the garage.

He would rest his head on 'The Little Prince,' which was permanently placed on Grandpa's lap.

Sniff around.

When Grandpa didn't react even to enthusiastic slobbery licks of his hand, I would bring peewee in from the garage or from the yard (since they had grown, we left the doors open for the pups). I would run his hand across her silky fur. And wouldn't stop until his gaze cleared.

Throughout the week, I was bothered mainly by one thing:

The phone.

It seldom rang.

With Dad's consent, apart from the family I liked the most—I invited two other families for Saturday.

Before the first arrived, Mom apologized again that she had better dedicate the limited time on her hands to Grandpa, who "isn't doing so great recently."

She approached the gate to introduce herself.

And went back to her affairs.

Sue came running.

Burst into the garage.

One after the other, she grabbed the pups.

The playful pups thought this was a new game, and kept running away.

Frantically she chased them around.

She barely even let the children come near.

Champion did not cooperate, either:

He refused to part from Grandpa.

"If Mohammed will not go to the mountain, the mountain will come to Mohammed"—I heard Mom saying to her father, and I couldn't tell if she was reprimanding him or joking with him, as I entered his room after the last of the guests had left. And she took advantage of my keeping him company by preparing dinner.

Once she left the room, with a trembling hand he put on his heavy-framed glasses. And with a hoarse voice he shared with me that Mom was "pretty impressed" with the first "candidates." And wondered whether I, too, thought they were interested in the little lady pup.

"Lad," I replied and laughed. "We already did this bit."

"Bit?" he wondered with a blank gaze.

I reminded him that he initially thought peewee was a male.

"Oh, well."

His expression betrayed distress and confusion.

Champion extended a leg.

And another one.

The chair rocked.

And Grandpa was startled.

"So: Mom was pretty impressed with the first candidates?" I repeated his words like an echo.

"The ones interested in the lady pup," he wouldn't budge. "They chose peewee…"

They're against spaying and they aren't interested in puppies, I explained. And from the very start they fell in love with the big one, and tied a blue ribbon around his neck. But they're still deliberating about

Nero, their elderly dog: what would be the most pleasant for him in his old age.

"There are thus two sides to a coin."

He eventually commenced with a somewhat enlivened voice:

"How does the bible go?

'…and honor the face of the old man'."

His voice trembled:

"And that is no trifle…

And we should not make light of it."

Dusting off his vocal cords, he was deeply moved by their consideration, which is by no means a common phenomenon in our world, especially in the modern age. But also in ancient times, when a life span was immeasurably shorter… Often… too often… unfortunately…

Loneliness and old age…

They are interdependent…

And what, according to our forefathers, is the remedy for the distress of old age? More than interested in asking, he seemed eager to reply, in his measured voice:

"Bringing a baby into the world—as the bible attests, 'Abraham and Sarah were old and well stricken in age,' when the barren Sarah was told that she had conceived our father Isaac, she laughed, 'After I am waxed old shall I have pleasure, my lord being old also?'

Or a young female spouse—as it is written about King David, who, when he was '**old and stricken in years**,'" emphasized the repetition of the phrase, "and in the way of elderlies, he suffered from chill, they brought a fair damsel to warm his body and to dispel the chill in his heart."

Dragging out even, shadow-elongating notes he mumbled that it is not inevitable that a puppy may serve as a combined cure, which will, little by little, dispel the loneliness… And breathe new life into the gloomy spirit of… of…

"Nero," I completed his sentence.

"Nero, may his darkness be lit…" he blurted out with a blank look.

"As to the old fellow—

There are two sides to a coin…

And only time will tell…"

I was also impressed by Yochi and Abraham who were crazy about dogs, and who were sent on a mission to the Ivory Coast, and whose children—Lihi, Itay and Yuval—were all grown up and lived on their own. And if there was anything they hated, it was returning to an empty house. And if Madam Lauren would confirm that they wouldn't suffer in the hot and humid climate, they would take two: the one with the green ribbon, and the one with the orange. And with a small voice I admitted that the third family—I wish I hadn't invited.

"Those who do not do, do not err."

He recited with a blank expression and dull eyes.

"No kidding…!"

Adi was impressed when I called her, mainly to find out how, in her opinion, Madam Lauren would respond.

"How should I know?!

The fact that she has dogs 'from the Ivory Coast to Japan,'" she quoted, "and that she's in touch with some of them, doesn't really tell us if she's also in touch with those in the Ivory Coast."

I went to sleep with butterflies in my stomach.

And woke up with them in the morning.

Upon my return from school, Sue scurried to the garage, and Champion—to Grandpa, who was sitting unbathed and unshaven, his glasses sliding down his nose, and on his knees 'The Little Prince,' opened to a random wrinkled page, as usual.

Champion rested his head.

Stuck his nose under the book.

Licked and licked.

And nothing…

I felt sorry for Sue, who was still showing signs of unrest, and returned empty-handed to Grandpa and Champion, who was curled up in the corner.

And every now and then rolled his eyes at him.

I served Grandpa lunch in his room.

Clicking his dentures like castanets, he opened and closed his mouth, even when the fork missed its destination.

"*Tsafra Tava*," he greeted me good morning in Aramaic, confused by the crow of Robert the rooster that had woken him up from his afternoon nap that had knocked him out in the rocking chair.

"You don't say…?!"

He was astounded that evening was approaching.

He staggered to the bathroom.

"Old Spice," he whispered when he returned on wobbly knees, embracing an opaque white bottle against his chest: "Your Grandmother's favorite scent."

At dinner, Mom didn't take her eyes off Champion, who wouldn't leave his side, and didn't accompany me even when I went to pick up the phone.

"Yay! Ruthie and Yehuda, Jonathan, Yalli, Gilya and Raphael are taking Don!" I announced excitedly.

"The one with the blue ribbon," I pointed at him so as to include Grandpa.

"Don, Don, Don," I repeated, ding-donging with the tip of my tongue against the roof of my mouth the name of the eldest of the pups and the first to be named.

And I rushed to call Adi to share the happy news.

"Let him be, please," Grandpa implored me when Champion refused to leave his side at night.

At noon, only Sue was waiting at the gate.

In the shuttered room Champion lay groveling at Grandpa's feet, while Grandpa repeatedly tried to catch something in the air that only he could see.

"Shhh… Shhh…"

I assumed he was cold.

So I covered him.

"Shhh… Shhh…"

He continued to point his finger, God knows at what.

"Do you want to shut the door?" I tried guessing. He shook his head.

Once he finished eating, he wiped his mouth with a napkin I had forgotten to give him.

Before waking him from his afternoon nap I closed the shutters and put on a bright light in the room, because I was under the impression that the evening hours extended his own twilight.

Thanks to this initiative, or perhaps unrelated to it, his confusion seemed less acute, and the fog of his mind dissipated with less effort.

In the evening he was exhausted. His eyelids drooped during a conversation about the first meeting between Nelson Mandela and the president of South Africa. Mom—who didn't take her eyes off Champion for a single moment—also viewed the meeting with de Klerk as an auspicious sign.

"**February eleventh, 1990** is a milestone in the war against the Apartheid!" Dad emphasized several months later, when, after twenty-seven years in prison, Mandela finally walked out a free man with a smile on his face.

"Lately, wherever you go, Champion follows…"

As if tapping against a tuning fork, Mom rushed to draw it near his ear. And she wondered why

Champion hadn't taken a special interest in Grandpa while Sue was busy with her affairs. Whereas now, when she is once again available, he prefers Grandpa's company to hers:

"Perhaps he has a score to settle with her…"

She cracked her knuckles.

"**Dogs**…" Dad's bushy eyebrows weighed down his large eyes that darkened as he stressed: "**never**… hold a grudge. It's part of what I love so much about **them**…"

Despite the great appreciation she held for Dad's empathy toward them, Mom felt that this was neither the time nor the place to settle disagreements that arise on occasion in every family.

"Certainly not out in the open…" she said with a soft, quiet tone, giving him a harsh and cautionary smile.

And once again she addressed her father, saying that lately, even during meals, Champion prefers his company even to my treats.

Dad shrugged.

Ran his fingers through his graying hair.

And his square jaw went up and down.

"C'est le ton qui fait la musique!"

Regaining his strength, Grandpa said nasally:

"It's the sound that makes the music!"

"I can't even remember the last time I managed to exchange a single word with her," Dad noted and continued with a businesslike tone:

"During the day—we're both at work.

At night—Tali collapses into bed.

And in between—she has no spare time. She has no energy. And she certainly has no patience for me."

"In my presence, kindly don't talk about me in the third person." More than imploring Dad, she warned him.

"For an incorrigible fixer there's no greater challenge than being confronted with helplessness and power-lessness," Dad explained in a low tone.

Next time, I promise to make every effort to be more available," Mom promised him.

"**Anything but that!**" he cried out.

"Anything but more effort," he suppressed his voice, "not for anyone. Not even for me!"

"All I meant to say was that I can't help but admire the way Champion treats Grandpa," she said, returning to the point she had made earlier.

"What can I say," Grandpa said with half a smile, "he, too, has fallen under my spell."

I leaped up at the rattle of the phone.

"That Madam is a real character," I repeated after Yochi and Abraham, who kept interrupting each other: "In a tropical climate black fur isn't optimal. And that means you can't let them run outside when it's very hot. But time will be at your disposal, and it's no problem. So we're saving two for you: the one with the orange ribbon, and the one with the green one."

Dad nodded in consent.

"Okay: so we'll wait for you this Friday, to come and pick up the two," I set the appointment with them.

When I returned to the table, Grandpa's eyelids were closed again.

We nearly carried him to bed in our arms.

Despite the late hour, I had to break the news to Adi. As if I wasn't the one who had called, she spoke a mile a minute: that very evening she happened to talk about the pups. It was a complete fluke her older brother stopped by, Idan, who, as I already knew, had recently returned from trekking all the jungles in South America, and for now was living with a roommate on Shenkin Street, in Tel Aviv. But he had already rented an apartment and was soon going to live on his own. I didn't understand what was going on with her: why did she think I would be interested in knowing where he lived and what a great job he had snagged because people considered him such a computer whiz?

"Wait," she kept going enthusiastically:

"That's not even the half of it!

Guess where he'll be working from?

You won't believe it…

From home!

And even a cell phone—they already gave him.

And the moment he heard about peewee…

You have no idea how psyched he became…"

I was choked with excitement.

But I played it cool.

"Like, hello, Ellie.

It's me, Adi.

Don't even dream about trying to fool me:

No one, no one's better than Idan.

We **hit the jackpot!**"

"Come on already," I heard him urging her, "tell her: **top dog handler**."

"I'm at your place in two minutes tops."

He informed me, having had enough of the Chinese whispers.

I explained Grandpa's situation to him and managed to hold off until the following day.

When I went to close Grandpa's door, Champion slipped out.

Even with him by me, I tossed and turned in bed until I fell asleep.

* * *

"Your dog is cranky as hell today,"

Idan greeted us the following day.

When the gate screeched against its hinge, Champion jumped on me.

And didn't stop barking.

He passed Adi.

Jumped on Idan.

And kept barking.

Sue greeted us with a restrained welcome.

As if going through the motions, she barked at Idan when Champion burst into the house.

Before I managed to enter the garage, he started barking again. I opened the door to Grandpa's room to let him in. And I rushed to join Adi and Idan, who gathered Sue and the pups. Shutting the doors to the kitchen and yard, he played with peewee and with Sue, while the others leaped at him.

Every now and then one of the pups burst into barks in a tenor that broke into a strident soprano.

To his call, he would kneel.

Look straight up.

And bark with a dexterity that wouldn't put any dog to shame.

Had it not been for Adi, I wouldn't have noticed Champion from a distance, barking in a hoarse baritone at us and the puppies.

He scratched the floor.

And almost knocked me over when he rose and sank his teeth into my sleeve.

"What is it?"

I petted him:

"Jealous?

Come on!"

The barks were replaced by moans that were no less firm.

"What do you want:

Food?

Water?

No problem."

Idan noticed this out of the corner of his eye:

"He's calling you. Can't you tell?"

I followed him.

"You want out?

Go out!"

I opened the door.

He crossed the threshold.

And did not stop barking while shaking his head oddly, spraying foam in every direction.

"Rony, go to Grandpa!"

He swung his tail from side to side.

And the barks chased and swallowed each other.

"Heel!"

He shook himself and obeyed.

We advanced together:

"Go in!

Come on already:

Go in!"

I urged him.

184

He remained standing like a beggar at the door.

I peeked in.
Rays of light passed through the slits between the shutters.

Gradually my eyes adjusted to the dimness.

And I noticed each item by itself:

The empty rocking chair.

The book on the seat.

The disheveled bed.

The dark window in the bathroom.

Champion raced from the door to the entrance.

And back again.

Dread crept up my spine.

As if possessed, I turned on the light:

Everything was exactly as it had been.

Only Grandpa…

Wasn't…

"What's going on?"

Idan startled me with a tap on the back:

"He's barking like crazy."

My head was empty:

"My grandfather's gone.

Like, vanished…"

I blurted out, petrified.

"Did you check upstairs?"

"**There's no reason to!**" I screamed, also to be heard above Champion's decibels.

"So it's not for nothing that he's so irritated today, your dog:

If your grandpa can barely move, we're off the hook.

Trust him: Champion will find him for you, for sure."

With his tail fluttering in the wind, Champion stormed the sidewalk.

He paused from time to time.

Sniffed a curbstone.

And charged forth.

Adi and I could barely keep up.

"You're in pretty poor shape, slowpokes," Idan goaded us.

Sweat trickled down.

186

Idan's shirt could have been wrung out.

Adi held her stomach when Champion stopped to sniff the behind of yet another of his kind.

"We'll end up finding some dog in heat," he joked.

Adi laughed.

I was not in the least amused.

Champion charged forth.

And covered a good distance.

Suddenly, he halted.

Waited alert on the curb.

Crossed the road at "heel."

And with high-pitched pants that became shorter and shorter, he continued to advance.

At the bus stop he paused again.

With unsteady feet and a foaming mouth he sniffed.

Wheezed.

And rolling his eyes, he plopped onto the sidewalk.

And did not get up.

"What's up with you?!

You think that if your grandpa goes missing it means that everything's gone to ruin.

Even Champion.

Don't worry:

It's just an epileptic fit," Idan diagnosed.

Panting, I told him about the "episode."

After making sure he wasn't on meds, he dismissed it in one fell swoop:

"A mild case.

What you would call a 'minor seizure.'"

I let Champion be.

And slowly slowly his normal breathing was restored.

"Then why isn't he getting up?"

I didn't understand.

"Maybe he's just wiped out, or he's out of leads," he said and laughed.

Meanwhile he fumbled for a pen.

And asked for Grandpa's phone number.

"What? You caught amnesia from him?!"

He waved the cell phone.

I was so frightened, my mind was hollow:

My memory was erased.

As if someone had pressed delete.

It took me a moment.

And yet, it came to me.

"Here, it's ringing."

He pressed the cell phone against my ear:

"You talk into this part."

He showed me.

"Ggg…rand…pa?"

Champion also pricked up his ear:

"…Where are you?!"

Tears choked my throat.

"What do you mean where am I?!

After all, you knew where to call!

The question is: where are you?

You were supposed to return a long time ago.

Why didn't you call immediately?"

"What do you mean where am I?!

What did you ask?!

Who did you ask it from?!"

"What do you mean?!" he wondered:

189

"In the note I wrote you."

"Note…?!

There was no note!"

I raised my voice.

"What do you mean?!

There most certainly was!" he stood his ground: "On top of the book, on the seat of the rocking chair—the first place you visit upon your return."

"You don't say?!"

He marveled at Champion's exploits:

"All the way to the station, huh…!

Unbelievable."

"So you missed the bus," I repeated after him so Adi and Idan would also hear. "And while you were pacing the pavement, a jeep pulled up beside you, driven by a pleasant-mannered woman, Mrs. Topaz—Shula, as Adi's mother asked that you address her. And Shula, who happened to be on her way to town, asked that you grant her the pleasure of driving you home."

He would not end the conversation before ensuring I kept this from Mom, and before I gave him my word that he would be the one to call her, and not me.

At home, they went straight to the garage.

And I—to Grandpa's room.

Champion followed me like a shadow.

When I bent down to scrape a crusted pulp of paper off the floor, he backed away.

And curled up in the corner.

"In our house we'd use the old Arabic saying to describe this: '*ili fat – mat*.' Meaning, 'what's passed, is dead,'" Idan said and laughed. He and Adi were now standing beside me, and with peewee cradled in his arms, he played with Sue who had pranced in after him.

"Good thing Champion understood the note he chewed…"

He looked me straight in the eye:

"And Andie—is it settled?"

He returned to the matter for which he had come.

Adi, who was worried he would name her Titi or Caca after the lake, guessed that it was from the Andes Mountains.

"Get a load of my sister: as smart as she is young, ha!" he melted with joy.

4

"We've had a dog's luck today…"

It was Dad who called. And he, who is always brief on the phone (even with Shlomo Zehavi), especially in the middle of a workday, insisted on hearing every detail about my conversation with Grandpa. And he grilled me about whether he had insinuated in any way, shape or form—directly or indirectly—that his departure was related to anything at all.

Shortly after, Mom stormed into the house.

"This time everything ended well. But it was your duty to inform me straight away. It's too heavy a responsibility for a child your age… you're not… heaven forbid, an orphan… We'll continue this conversation on the way," she blurted, and went to pack Grandpa's medicine and vitamins.

When she opened the car door for him, Champion leaped in.

I, too, was surprised by the invitation to sit in the front seat:

"It's time that for once we had an uninterrupted conversation."

Cold wind blew in through the half-open window, and Mom turned on the heat.

"A car is like a little house. Right?"

She smiled as if letting me in on a secret.

At the traffic light she wrung her hands:

"My father, I believe I know pretty well," she began, and as if she had been present during the conversation, she recounted it, including the note.

"If so, let's ask ourselves: why, in your opinion, did he choose to return home today of all days. Not yesterday, or the day before, or any other day?" she asked, tapping out her words with her wedding ring against the steering wheel.

"Since he stopped following the pups he doesn't have anything to do at our place," I replied. And in the same breath I added that lately, she hasn't been into them either. She won't even answer the phone.

"If that's the case, the question must be asked: why did he choose to leave today, of all days?"

Since I didn't reply, she hinted:

"Perhaps something preceded his departure?"

Due to the way Dad grilled me earlier, I raised the possibility that maybe it had something to do with the conversation from the previous night.

"And how?"

"Maybe he felt kind of bad that Dad didn't agree with you about Sue and Champion."

At the mention of his name, he licked my neck.

And went back to his lookout post.

"You're almost there.

Warmer."

As if we were playing 'hot or cold,' she guided me by accelerating the rhythm of her taps. And admitted that lately she had become concerned that Champion—with his healthy instincts—had noticed a decline in Grandpa's condition.

Champion didn't deprive her, either.

And remained sitting between her erect neck and the backrest of my seat.

I told her how he acts when Grandpa is confused.

She removed one hand from the steering wheel and straightened out her skirt:

"Mountains out of molehills…

Mountains out of molehills…"

She repeated like a broken record.

When she sees "molehills," she explained, it is a sure sign that somewhere, "mountains" are lurking—even if no one but her has noticed them yet.

"In the future don't hide such things from me!" she ordered with a harsh softness.

"You're not exactly forthcoming with me either…"

Her eyes gaped wide.

"You barely…

Barely…

Even…

Even…

Tell me…

That your head hurts."

I found a way to blur the traces of my eavesdropping.

Rubbing her forehead as if beckoning a decision, she mumbled:

"There's a Jewish saying that goes: 'One generation shall pass word on to the next.'

Whereas in our case: one generation shall pass on muteness to the next…"

And for the third time she asked me to tell her:

"What's the connection between the conversation and the timing?"

And she continued to straighten out her skirt, shrouding herself in silence.

At the traffic light, she stopped.

Her eyes fixed on the road opening ahead, but her gaze turned inward.

She patted her thigh as if reaching a decision:

"Ellienka," she began with a hesitant voice, "today I want to talk to you about something we've never discussed."

She paused.

"This is quite a difficult conversation.

It isn't easy for me to talk about it.

And I'm asking you in advance to forgive me if this saddens you: we never spoke about my mother. All you know from me is that 'what happened, happened' before you were born.

I never told you, for instance, that when what happened to us happened, I stopped believing in vows.

And I haven't made a single vow since, except for one…

I also never told you, for example, that when what happened to us happened, I lost the joy of life.

More precisely: even when I was happy, my heart was not light.

I was not really happy.

Not completely.

Not like before.

At some point, and I'm not sure when, I stopped believing that I would ever feel happiness again.

That was the situation.

And I got accustomed to it.

All this was true until you, Ellienka, came into the world.

You reconnected me to happiness.

No less.

Needless to say that the last thing I wanted—that I'd ever want—is to make you sad.

I watched you then, when you were born, and my heart swelled.

I thought about my mom, of course.

But I only thought about how happy she would have been with you.

And that very moment, I vowed never to talk to you about this until you turned nine. As you've heard from Grandpa, that was my age when I lost my mom.

For a brief moment she took her eyes off the road.

Glanced at me.

And as if to sweeten a bitter pill, she asked me to take out the small bag of candy from her purse and treat us both to one.

She sucked.

Took a deep breath.

And with a mouth that was no longer dry, Mom—who in any state of mind devotes herself to her work in the garden—spoke nostalgically of the "deep-rooted evergreen oak," in the shade of which she took shelter as a child: "A tree that is considered immortal," she explained to me, "even the strongest wind can't overpower, both because of its thick trunk and its branches that create a round treetop, resistant to pests."

For a brief moment she studied my expression.

And stared straight ahead again.

Focused on the road, with reserved emotion she described her mother as a loving, interested, involved, attentive, understanding and non-judgmental mother, with a sense of humor and great resourcefulness. A woman who was her best friend, and her husband's best friend. A beautiful, warmhearted, wise, kind, intelligent, gentle and talented woman. Creative, especially at interpersonal relations. Industrious and successful, at work as well. Even with her placating nature, she knew exactly when to stand her ground. She had a refined taste in culture and loved music, especially the guitar. A healthy woman, who, as far as she can remember, never even got the flu, who presided over the family with amicability, openness, sensitivity and joie de vivre.

Everything flowed peacefully.

Always smooth sailing.

And then, one day, on her way back from work, she didn't feel well.

She threw up.

And the moment she arrived home, she asked her to call Grandpa.

Grandpa arrived right away.

Following him—the ambulance.

Nine days he spent with her at the hospital.

And every morning a note waited for her on the pillow:

Good morning Talinka,

I arrived late.

And you were already asleep.

Sara'le ("my nanny when I was little," Mom explained to me) will arrive at seven to take you to school.

Mom's condition is improving.

Slowly, but surely.

Just a little more patience.

I will send her your regards today as well,

I will kiss her for you,

I will wish her a swift recovery on your behalf,

And I will tell her you miss her and await her return.

On the ninth evening he returned early.

Under his arm was a small bundle.

He stood at the threshold as if he didn't know what to do with it.

Eventually he took the bundle into the bedroom.

Went out to the car again.

And returned with the gramophone and records.

When he put them down, she noticed her mother's watch, which looked funny on his hairy wrist.

With a heartbreaking look he asked Sara'le the nanny to stay and prepare dinner for her.

And even when she left, he uttered not a single word:

"He didn't have the heart to.

Nor could he find the words."

Before bedtime, as if collecting himself:

There was no way to make it easier…

Telling her what he had to tell her.

Mom loved her to no end.

Infinitely.

There was no one Mom loved as much as her.

And there was no one who made her as happy as she did.

Mom had whom to live for.

She had what to live for.

She was very sick…

More than he imagined…

And she sank…
Into… a deep sleep.

But… it wasn't sleep.
It was a deep coma…
A coma…

He believed
He was convinced
That she would wake up.

And that once she woke up
She would return to herself.

He did not lose hope for a moment.

There were also signs
Somewhat encouraging.

With a voice as if from the grave he mumbled:
This morning…
There was…
A deterioration…

What happened, happened…
Mom didn't wake up…

And Mom won't wake up…

Ever…

Mom is gone.

Mom is dead.

Passed away.

Mom will no longer be with us:

Not today.

And not tomorrow.

And not ever.

But she will always, always…

Stay with us:

In our hearts.

In our memories.

And occasionally—in our dreams.

It was someone else's mother he spoke about:

Her mother

Has a headache.

Nausea.

Vomiting.

And that passes.

Her mother was not in a deep coma.

If she was, he wouldn't have sent her regards and get well wishes from her.

Her mother would soon recover, just as he had written her.

Return home.

And everything would go back to being as it was.

Her father didn't take back his words.

And the despondency.

The horrible pallor.

And the depths of sadness in his eyes.

Slowly slowly, bit by bit, something began to seep in.

"And even when the lightening cleft the core of the oak. Burned the dark green off. And shed the splendor of its catkin blossoms, it took me years…

Many years…

Until I started to internalize the finiteness…"

Now, as before, I cannot imagine a book-lover like Grandpa, lying in bed day and night like an "unwanted object."

And what did Mom gather from this?

That for her he finds no reason to get out of bed in the morning.

And as her mother used to say: "That is a feeling she would not wish even upon the worst of her enemies."

A horrible fear befell her…

That she would lose him too…

Over time—with extreme effort—he began to get up when she did.

Send her off to school.

And the moment the door slammed shut behind her, he would return to bed, as she discovered one morning, when she came back to retrieve a notebook.

The bed was a magnet:

There she would find him upon her return as well.

Unbathed.

And unshaven.

Eating—he was unable to.

And from one day to the next he became thinner and thinner.

With time, the bed began to lose its gravitational force.

Even though he struggled with it anew each morning.

And his efforts were not always met with the same measure of success…

More than a month passed, until one day she returned from school.

And found him dressed.

And his beard shaved.

He cleaned and tidied the apartment as well.

Even the bed was not disheveled.

After a while, he crossed the threshold for the first time.

And went to get his hair cut.

At first he visited only nearby shops.

And gradually expanded his radius.

Food—he bought prepared.

Once he cooked us our first meal, he returned to work.

Nothing went back to being as it was.

But from then on, her father was always at her side:

In any matter, big or small.

The grief did not fade.

Grief has no expiration date.

Each of us buried it deep inside.

As though it was his very own private "little temple."

It exists.

It lives.

It breathes.

The twinge in the heart becomes an inseparable part of you.

You learn to live with it.

And to move on.

Forward.

The loneliness didn't go away, either.

Nor did the longing—

Not his.

And not mine.

On the contrary, they, too, became permanent companions.

"Elliek." She, my green-thumbed mother, whispered my pet name with an introverted softness, which has since become reserved for special occasions, "despite the lightning that struck it and burned it nearly to its roots. And despite the downpour that followed and flooded it—the evergreen oak didn't become a bare tombstone. What spared it was the fertile soil, the deep roots it struck, the pure water, the thoroughly arable land, and the fine nutrients it managed to accumulate over nine years, which in hindsight are nothing but the blink of an eye.

And when the tissues of the xylem started growing back and the phloem bloomed once again, the blossoms encompassed the scars and covered them, until they were barely discernable."

Her gaze was "lost in the distance," as I imagine the gaze of the Little Prince when he decided to disappear.

"Elliek, this is a lot to take in.

I can only hope that I didn't make you sadder than candor necessitates."

Once again she took a deep breath.

And after a long pause, Mom, who like the Little Prince never forgets a question once she asks it, returned for the umpteenth time to the question she had posed about Grandpa. Only this time she was convinced that it was superfluous for her to explain to me why, after the previous night's conversation in the kitchen, she was so alarmed about what would happen, which is exactly what did happen, that she couldn't sleep a wink all night.

Even now, from a distance of time and place, containing it—consumes all my mental strength.

And I need a respite.

"It is only with the heart that one can see rightly.

What is essential is invisible to the eye.

It is only with the heart that one can see rightly.

What is essential is invisible to the eye.

See rightly…

Invisible to the eye …

It is only with the heart that one can see…

It is only with the heart that one can …

It is only with the heart …

It is only with the heart that one can see rightly.

What is essential is invisible to the eye.

What is essential…

What is essential…

Essential…

Invisible to the eye…

Invisible…

Invisible…

Only with the heart…

What is essential is invisible…

It is only with the heart that one can see rightly.

What is essential is invisible to the eye."

Countless variations play inside me.

And I laugh deep inside at the thought that one of the most meaningful sayings, if not the most meaningful in 'The Little Prince'—Antoine de Saint-Exupéry chose to put in the mouth of the fox, of all characters.

And I leave the fox to his guile.

And return to Champion, who had become restless from the busy traffic, which he was not used to, on Namir Road close to HaKirya military base, as we drove into the city of Tel-Aviv.

I reached back.

And petted him until he calmed down.

"So that's what Grandpa meant by 'once bitten, twice shy'?"

I asked to make sure.

"Literally speaking, it feels more like a burn than a bite. Like anesthetized tissue," she replied and nodded.

And hesitantly asked me to tell her "in all honesty":

What does separation mean to me?

"Simple: it's just like with the puppies that are going to leave us. And in their new homes they'll be just as happy as they are in ours."

Mom let out a sigh of relief.

And laughed a glowing laughter, as I had never heard her laugh before.

"And what does it mean to you?"

I insisted on knowing.

"To me…

To me…

For my part…

And likely for Grandpa's as well…"

As if searching for the right tone.

And once she found it, she did not hold back: The moment the decision was made to find new homes for the pups, they're gone.

And she misses them.

She would have wanted to pet them.

And can't.

"And you could rightfully ask me:

Why?

For one very simple reason: For me, and most likely for Grandpa as well, they were here and now they're gone."

I, who find this too complicated even today, wondered:

"If that's the case, then why do you keep parking on the street and carrying bags and get soaking wet instead of just parking in the garage?

You do it because you know as well as I do that the puppies are running around in there!"

I answered my own question.

"I know that here,"

She tapped a finger against her temple.

"But not here,"

She pounded on her chest.

I didn't understand a thing.

"Imagine that you're at the amusement park," she said, laughing. "And you're trying to scratch the tip of your nose by its reflection in a distorting mirror."

That didn't help, either.

"There's an external reality, and an internal one," she tried again:

"There's a practical reality, and an emotional one." I understood only one thing:

That out of fear, she's separating for no reason.

For no reason at all.

"Not exactly: you fear something defined.

In my case, and I'm positive that in Grandpa's case as well, I'd say one thing:

For some people the cure takes precedence over the blow, and for some, like me, for instance, the blow takes precedence over the cure."

"So what about the pups in the meantime?"

I lost hope of understanding.

"In the meantime—the between time—that's all I'm capable of."

She smiled despondently:

"Practically, the pups are here. And I take care of their food and the rest of their needs. Emotionally, they're long gone."

* * *

If not for the barks of joy, I wouldn't have noticed that she had parked.

Mom opened the door for him.

Champion leaped out.

Next to the lamppost he raised a leg.

And still dripping, he rushed to push on the iron gate, which swung squeakily on its hinge.

With a perked tail he raced along the path.

Pushed the latticed glass door.

And I followed him into the tall and narrow entrance hall, which was flooded with a blanching neon light even during the day.

Wagging, he ran forward.

And returned with his tail between his legs.

Clung to my left.

And in a hesitant "heel" he once again crossed the painted tiles.

At the front of the staircase he paused.

Prostrated himself.

And the iron railing hummed from the loud volume of his barks and their frequency.

It was clear to me that one of the neighbors would arrive any moment.

But it was a ghost house.

The barks left no doubt that he was caught between the physical proximity to Grandpa and an acute case of stair anxiety.

"It's stronger than him."

The vibrations in Mom's voice were ominous.

Nothing helped.

With no other choice, I dragged him by the collar.

Once he made it across the first part of the staircase, he charged ahead like a terrified panther.

He stopped on Grandpa's doorstep.

Breathless, Mom caught up with us:

"Tighten the collar, so he won't knock Grandpa over, heaven forbid." Before sticking the key into the lock she began giving orders:

"Wait until I sit him down!

Wait until I place Grandma's trinkets on a high shelf, so he won't fling them with his tail! And only then let him in!"

I hadn't noticed that I was leaning against the doorbell.

And I didn't understand who was ringing.

Grandpa waited on the other side of the door.

And opened.

With bristling fur, Champion growled oddly.

His tail stretched out and swayed like the pendulum of a metronome from one side to the other in measured beats.

He spread his legs and sprawled onto the floor.

Crawled a few centimeters to the rattling sound of the links of his collar.

Licked Grandpa's shoe.

And another one.

"I am grateful for your visit."

His voice disclosed his emotional state when he cordially invited him in.

He carried on his licking.

"Sit!"

I commanded.

He stopped licking.

And obeyed.

"Heel!"

He sprawled and went back to licking.

"Free!"

I ordered.

Mom and I tried to drag him by pulling the doormat.

He bared his teeth and growled in warning.

"His blocking your way with his body," she said and laughed.

"Are you, ladies, also waiting for a special invitation?" Grandpa wondered.

"You've really driven us crazy today," I whispered in his ear as I passed by him.

A spark of youthful mischief lit up his eyes.

And as quickly faded.

With Mom supporting his arm, Grandpa shuffled into the guest room.

Champion didn't bat an eye.

He didn't even peep inside, into the apartment he hadn't been to in years.

Nor did he make eye contact.

"Now you are my guests.

And I will treat you to whatever your hearts desire.

What do you desire?"

He set the tone.

He offered me whipped chocolate milk, who no one makes like he used to.

He offered Mom Turkish coffee, "With a touch of cardamom, a-la-Dad, and kaymak, clotted cream, he translated from Turkish, the spécialité de la maison," he flaunted the amalgam of languages.

Mom's offer to accompany him—he rejected.

My offer to keep him company—he accepted.

And barely dragged his feet as we walked together.

I had been in his kitchen countless times. And I was always deterred by the neglect, the abandonment, the infirmity, the decay, the damp, the viscous loneliness.

Arm in arm, we entered the era of Grandma Michaela, when the space was the beating heart of a loving and lively family, and which was preserved just as it had been:

With the same old burner of cracked grayish enamel;

The same oil-stained counter, damaged and unstable;

Same oven and the same washing machine in the utility balcony;

Same rattling, sweating refrigerator;

Same closets and same airing cupboard with its heavy doors and loose hinges, and with the same injured red plastic knobs, which no longer bore evidence of their once round shape; same rectangular formica table with the meringue-like pattern, attached to the wall; same three wooden chairs with their frayed and cracked upholstery, which had once been red, pushed against it.

From the dust-riddled lace curtains to the greasy pastel-colored floral oilcloths, furled on the ill-planed shelves—everything had the blood-curdling touch of distant years, during which Grandma Michaela had managed her household, years which I knew so little about.

Champion eagerly gulped down the water I served him.

I returned to the kitchen.

Opened the fridge.

And my heart sank: among the moldy dairy products and rotting fruit and vegetables, changing their states of matter, fresh products poked out here and there.

I tossed out a curdled yogurt.

Cheese growing furry mold.

The corpses of putrid fruit and vegetables.

At his request, I closed the door to the kitchen.

As though seeking refuge, Grandpa held onto the counter as if seizing the horns of the altar.

To the spine-tingling grating of rusty hinges, with a trembling hand he took out of the oven a cinnamon cake and sweet pastries, whose appearance attested to their freshness:

"As long as we have cakes." He moved on to everyday matters.

With a shaking hand he filled a cup.

And the water spilled from his tremors.

And he measured once again.

And the coffee grinds spilled as well.

And he once again counted teaspoons.

And the stove burner wouldn't obey him, either:

It refused to turn on.

Eventually he let me light it.

Even though the door was closed, he lowered his voice:

"Unlike Bialik, our national poet, who wrote:

'I didn't stumble on light left abandoned…'

I can testify to the contrary:

'I did stumble on light left abandoned...'

All of you—Mom, Dad, you and Champion—were model hosts."

He waited.
And once I gave him my word that everything would remain the way it was between us, he didn't withhold: "In the winter of my life, all I wish is not to be a burden on anyone. And certainly not on my daughter."

He cleared his throat.
And mumbled:

"Thou hast enticed me… and I was enticed,

Thou hast overcome me, and hast prevailed…"

As if encouraging himself.

In hindsight I am in awe of how easily he skipped over two thousand and six hundred years, and tried to draw strength from the words of the persecuted prophet, when he complained that I was making him say more than he intended to…

He focused on the coffee, which almost spilled over.

And continued to stare at it even after I turned off the flame.

The hand he leaned on trembled.

And he began losing his balance.

I helped him sit.

And he continued to hold his tongue.

"Shh…

Shhhh… "

He held his finger against his lips.

"Shh…

Shhh…

Shhhh…"

He silenced himself.

When I once again gave him my word, as though against his better judgement, he reluctantly carried on:

"It is not easy at any age to keep one's head above water. And the older you become the more effort it takes: every now and then there are aches. And it takes longer to oil one's legs in the morning and put them into gear, or half gear," he chuckled. "And sometimes your head is slightly dizzy. Every now and then your memory betrays you as well." But as long as the engine is more or less in order, he does not see the point in excessive commotion. And even when it starts to be slightly off, it doesn't necessarily mean one should start rushing from doctor to doctor like a drugged mouse. "One should worry when the time comes…"

At his age, he was "steadfast" about "making the best and the most" out of what he still hoped, that evening, life may throw his way. And he was determined not to be "a burden on anyone." And certainly not on his daughter, who had just recently started living:

For her, "The path still stretches on long and wide."

And he made me swear that when I grew older I would read the writings of that poet with the perceptive eye and the bewitching talent, who wrote about the stretching road.

"What is there for me to I say?!

As the Talmud goes:

'Woe to me if I do it,

Woe to me if I do not.'"

He groaned.

Champion, the gatekeeper, hardly flinched when we slowly made our way back to the living room. Nor did he move when I pushed the groaning tea cart, in the center of which stood the metal coffee pot with its long handle.

Grandpa sipped his coffee in silence.

Sunk deeper into the armchair.

And dozed off.

At Mom's request, Dad came to pick up me and Champion on his way home from work, and almost carried Grandpa to bed in his arms.

That night Mom slept at his house.

Early in the morning she called to break the bad news: "Grand...pa... we...nt... to... sleep...

And... didn't... wake... up..."

She sobbed:

"His... heart...

Sto...pped..."

"A merciful death.

A righteous man's death," Dad mumbled.

* * *

Now, when the "adequate mental space" has been found, the voices and the silences play within me, and weave the fibers of my soul warp and weft. And I see the silences stretching from Grandpa to Mom, and from Mom to me.

More attuned and attentive than ever before, I wait until the echo of the last chord fades.

Silence.

Complete stillness.

There is not a trace of a single cell of an echo foreign to the texture.

I stretch.

Open my eyes.

And it isn't the light in the floor lamp that's growing pale.

Nor is it the beam of the spotlight that's dimming.

It is the twilight of the dawn that's breaking.

I put down my baton.

And walk off the stage.

Made in the USA
Coppell, TX
10 July 2023

18947351R00125